Als

Warrior

WARRIOR

CROSSFIRE SERIES BOOK FIVE

by

GENNITA LOW

To Father and Mother

Ranger Buddy, my Warrior Friend

Stash, my Secret Warrior

Dedicated to all the warriors, those in the
crossfire,
who bravely served or are serving.

Special thanks to Sandy Stills who witnessed the
birth of Cumber
in the pink room and Karen King for copy editing.

PART ONE

CHAPTER ONE

He could hear the story being passed around his team now. The Stooges pretty in pink. The Stooges spent a night together on a pink four-poster bed. The Stooges had pink bathrobes and slippers.

"Ya gotta admit, Cumber, pink is sexy."

"I prefer them on my women, hidden away for my pleasure," he said.

"True, but maybe this room was meant to be inspiring, right, Dirk?"

"Mink, if you're sporting a boner, you get to sleep on the floor."

Lucas Branson, AKA Cucumber by his SEAL team mates, came from a family of warriors. His father was an Airborne Ranger of the 173rd, the biggest, baddest fighting group of men ever. His cousins were scattered around the world, playing war games in special operations and doing what warriors do best, bringing down the enemy. He came from a family of tall men, big hulks descended from, as his father liked to tell him when he was a kid, giants who ruled the earth. And he'd grown up believing his father as he grew up towering over shorter men and taking lessons to become the next warrior-in-line in a family fueled by competition and medals.

And now he was a SEAL, the U.S. Navy's special operations force specializing in sea, air and land where the biggest, baddest group of boys resided. His team mates were his best friends and part of the family, and he didn't let anybody get to him. They called him Cucumber— Cumber for short—because he always kept his cool, no matter the situation.

But not tonight. Tonight, he was thinking about killing his sister. He loved her very, very much, but yeah, he might just strangle her.

He stared up at the bright pink canopy above him with its frilly lace and big bows and drooping flowery shit with children's faces inside them, all smiling down on the bed's occupants. Strings of pink pearls dangled, waving gently.

It had to be a slow death. Because he knew she was laughing her ass off right now. A slow, painful..."

"Hey, Cumber, how big is your dick?"

"I'm in a fucking pink bed with two men in a fucking pink room. My head is resting on a fucking pink pillow the shape of a pink flamingo. I'm not discussing my dick with you."

"But what else can you talk about on a pink bed in a pink room?" Dirk insisted. "Unless you want to chitchat about the pearls and bows. Or the cupids around the pink mirror. I was mesmerized by them while using the pink hairdryer."

Mink sighed loudly. "I need a dose of manhood. Let's talk about Cumber's dick. A huge dick should cure us from an overdose of estrogen. Come on, Cumber, how big is your dick?"

Lucas ignored his friends. His sister...what was the best way for revenge? Maybe he could sit on her till she begged for mercy. Except, she had a black belt and as a big brother, he'd taught her quite a few moves to protect herself. He used to hide her favorite toy, but at their age he needed something a bit more...painful.

"You know he's got the biggest dick of all of us," Dirk said, "so why the need to know?"

"If it's so damn big, why didn't he have the balls to say no to the Pink Room?"

Lucas closed his eyes as his two friends, having made their point, roared out laughing. They were very close buddies—they were often called the Stooges—so close they could ad lib a whole comedy routine without a script on the spot. He'd known one was coming the moment they'd stepped into the Pink Room, the "most popular" suite at his aunt's B&B.

The laughter went on for a good minute, till his friends were holding their stomachs and choking. He lay there, waiting for it to subside. He could turn on the TV, except holding on to a pink sparkly remote would just set them off again. He stared resolutely at his feet at the end of the bed, peeking out of the dark pink comforter. Yeah, if he had time, he'd sew up Lulu's sleeping bag so the next time she went out camping, she would get a nice surprise when she tried to crawl in and stretch out after a long day hiking. Except that kind of revenge took too long to realize. He wanted to get back at her *now*.

"You know, Cumber," Dirk finally gasped out, "when she said, 'The Pink Room will be perfect for you and your gentlemen friends to relax in,' I was having visions of your stately aunt being the madam of a secret boudoir, especially when she added, 'You'll find lots in the room for entertainment. Enjoy yourselves, boys!' I thought maybe she was pulling our legs or something. I never expected *this*!"

Dirk spread his arms out to include the whole room. Mink, lying in the middle, pushed one arm away.

"Watch it. You're encroaching on my pink space."

"Yeah. She gave us one four-poster bed, dude," Dirk continued. "What was she thinking?"

"The place is booked up. This was the only suite available," Lucas said. "My aunt probably thought we would be happy with the biggest room she could put us in."

"Man, didn't she know we sleep on submarines? We can crawl in one of her closets and take our naps there," Mink said.

"Yeah, but we wouldn't be tucked in and enjoying our pink featherbeds, yo."

"Look, I know you two are doing me a favor using our time off to help my aunt and sis move furniture, so I'm taking your digs without retaliation," Lucas said, affecting a yawn. "What's the big deal? Just fucking close your eyes and pretend you're lying in a muddy river already. Me? A bed is a bed. We'll be out of this place in two days, tops. Then we can go party somewhere for 24 hours before we head back. Now turn off the damn lights."

"I can't. I need a drink first to get the smiling pink cherubs from haunting my dreams tonight."

"Cucumber, go get us a drink. You owe us. The pink fridge is at your side of the bed, anyway. And oh, the pink bottle opener is hanging..."

The sound of the door unlocking cut off the rest of Mink's sentence. Lucas turned his head, full attention on the door. Someone outside kicked it wide open. His sister popped her head in and a big flash blinded him.

"Surprise, pink SEALs!" He heard her yell out as she ran off. "Picture is on 'My Friends Space' page!"

Lucas jumped off the bed and chased the shadowy figure as she made off, laughing, down the corridor. He heard Mink and Dirk behind him, following along.

Must get back that camera.

Must. Kill. Sister.

The B&B was a big mansion, with many hiding places. His sister, like Lucas and his team, was barefoot, her feet making barely a sound as she climbed the stairs. He took the steps three at a time, hoping they wouldn't creak too much. The chase must be done on the quiet. They had their aunt to consider. And the guests, too.

Going up was good. That meant she was heading to the private section, away from the guests. The only obstacle was his aunt's apartment also being up here, so if his sister managed to slip in there before he got to her, she would be home free. No way was he going to bother his sleeping aunt, what with him and his team mates shirtless and wearing only shorts...shit...he just remembered Mink had only his underwear on. Fuck. Please God, don't let Aunt Clementine walk out of her rooms. Because he didn't want to explain to the family how a naked SEAL buddy sent their proper, very Southern aunt into a conniption fit in the middle of the night.

Out of the corner of his eye, he saw Mink in his tighty whities scaling to the next story using the wooden banisters. With him snapping at her heels and Mink cutting off her escape route, his sister was going to be trapped between them any moment now. She reached the top of the landing, saw her problem, tried to dive through Mink's legs, got tangled and up-ended him. Lucas heard muffled ouches and oomph's as he reached them. He took a step nearer to apprehend their target.

A door suddenly opened and a shadowy figure jumped on top of Lucas' back with a "Hoo-ah!," startling all four of them who were already out there. A puny arm curled around his neck, trying to force him back. The new attacker weighed less than a sack of flour but Lucas realized Dirk, who was covering his six, wouldn't know that. Not wanting to hurt his sister's sidekick, he curled his arms under the assailant's knees, twisted sideways against the corridor wall and sat down, thus imprisoning the assailant. One thing registered quickly. Whoever it was had very nice, silky smooth, bare legs, which were now paddling hard like a panicked creature, trying to kick him. The puny hand around his neck reached down and grabbed a handful of his chest hair.

"Ow!" Lucas growled, tugging at the hand. He slid his hands up from under his prisoner's knees and grabbed a handful of silky smooth ass. His assailant squealed.

"Get off, you goof!" He heard his sister's demand coming from a few feet away.

"No way," came Mink's reply. "I think you have something that belongs to..."

Another door opened. The landing was suddenly flooded with light. Cucumber blinked. Everyone froze.

"Lucas Samson and Lucille Belle Branson! What's going on out here? Oh my goodness! Mr. Mink!"

Lucas closed his eyes. Aunt Clementine in curlers and pearls. Definitely a sight that would doom any warrior's rage.

***

In hindsight, Kit admitted she shouldn't have run out of her room, yelling "Hoo...ah!" at the top of her lungs, and jump on a big SEAL. And was he big. Lulu had said her brother was much taller, and Lulu was almost six feet tall. Lucas Branson wasn't only taller, but he was broader too. Riding on his back felt like she was mounting her uncle's prized bull, and one whose bare back she was squished against and tasting right now.

Her hand, lost somewhere around his chest area, found hair. She pulled hard.

"Ow!"

In retaliation, a big hand cupped her rump and squeezed. She squealed and took a bite at the naked back. Argh. What was the man made of, granite?

She heard muffled voices—one of them Lulu's—and tried to peer from behind the warm body...how many of these guys were there? Lulu had told her over the phone she had a mission to prank her brother tonight, but she'd thought he was here alone. When she'd arrived, Lulu was already in excitement mode and ready to make her move, giving her the bare-bones details of her plan as she made off with a flashlight and her phone.

Right now, it sounded like a game of twister going on, with body parts squished and tangled and people making noises. Suddenly, the hall light came on.

"Lucas Samson and Lucille Belle Branson! What's going on out here? Oh my goodness! Mr. Mink!"

Oh-oh. It was Miss Clementine. Eeek.

The hard body holding her prisoner shifted, although, she noted, his hand was still grasping her ass. A low male voice rumbled through the wall of flesh.

"Sorry, Aunt Clementine. Why don't you...uh...go back to bed? We'll straighten up out here."

"But why are you all on the floor outside my rooms? And why is Mr. Mink without any pants on?"

What? Kit tried to budge the muscled wall trapping her. One of them is naked? And Miss Clementine got to see him and she didn't? *Move, you lug head, move!*

"I'm sorry, Miss Clementine, truly," she heard another male voice say, sounding slightly sheepish.

"I think you should get off Lucille and make yourself decent, Mr. Mink. And I may be old but I can see your hands hanging off my banister, Mr. Dirk. How long do you think you can hide like that without falling and causing damage to my staircase, young man?"

There was a small pause. Then a creak and a thud.

"Sorry, Miss Clementine." The third male voice sounded meek. "It's all Cucum...I mean, Lucas', fault."

"I will get to him in a moment. Miss Kit-Ling, is that you behind Lucas?"

Oh, now she was in deep doo-doo. Miss Clementine was going to be aghast at her attire. She moved her head, resting her cheek on the back-that-would-not-move.

"Yes, it's me," she replied. "I can explain, really."

"Lucas, can you tell me why you're sitting on Miss Kit-Ling? I don't even think you've met."

Finally, the-back-that-would-not-move came alive. It shifted, giving her some space.

"We...just met, Aunt Clementine," that deep voice rumbled. "It was just an accident. It was dark and someone fell and we all sort of tried to catch Lulu quietly so she wouldn't wake you up. Totally failed operation, that's all. It was actually all Lulu's fault."

"Hey, don't get me in trouble," Lulu protested.

"You started it!"

"You didn't have to send your boys to do the dirty work of...oh, I give up. Aunt Clementine, go to bed. It's my fault. I tripped and fell."

"Humph. That doesn't explain the inappropriate attire. You're all acting like..." There was a soft sigh. "We courted differently in my days, that's all. I'm going back to bed.

We'll have a talk in the morning. Can I expect better attire?"

"Yes, ma'am," everyone mumbled.

Kit cocked her head, listening. When she heard Aunt Clementine's soft footsteps move through her doorway, which then clicked shut, she tapped Mr. Granite-Back on the shoulder.

"Oh yeah, I keep forgetting about the spider I'm squashing," Lucas mocked, getting up.

Air. She took a deep breath. Goodness, that body was hot. She blinked and looked up at the whole man. Miles and miles of man. She exhaled loudly. *Oh, my goodness. That body. Was. H-h-hot.*

She'd seen Lulu's brother in some photos before. Graduation, some camping trip with Lulu's family, a bearded and scruffy guy with a backpack—she hadn't really paid much attention. Her own father and brothers were Airborne Rangers, so she'd seen enough military guys not to notice much beyond their short haircuts, neat uniforms and tendency for machismo. Lucas Branson was just a name, her friend's brother who was in the navy.

However, Lucas Branson in person? Wow.

There were miles of legs to admire. And above those shorts, a narrow waist that broadened into a hairy chest. Whose hairs she'd pulled. She tilted her head back and met a pair of amused eyes.

"You thinking of sleeping there tonight?"

Dammit. He'd caught her looking. His hand was extended, offering to help her up. She placed hers in his. He pulled her onto her feet with ease.

"I was catching my breath," she explained huffily. "Something heavy was cutting off all my air."

"I wasn't leaning back too hard," he said. "Besides, you bit me."

"You pinched my..." She cut off the word "ass" and looked around. "...me. Oh, no wonder Miss Clementine sounded so horrified."

There was a mostly naked SEAL on top of Lulu. And he was holding her down as if he was never going to let go. He

13

was smiling down at her friend, though, who was looking spitting mad.

A flash of light. Kit turned her head. Another man was standing by the stairs with his smart phone in one hand.

"Yeah, tit for tat. Now if she posts, we can put this pic up."

"Ha, you think that's going to scare me off putting up a pic of three SEALs snuggling in a pink bed?"

"Maybe we should dangle her by her feet over the banisters. That should be scary enough," Mink suggested. "What do you say, Cucumber? Permission to dangle your sister till she cries for mercy, sir!"

Kit blinked. *Cucumber?*

She glanced back at the man beside her and suddenly realized he was still holding her hand. And also looking at her as if he wasn't going to let go. Something dropped like an anchor in her gut.

"You do what you have to, Mink," Lucas said, his gaze still holding Kit's, "although I suggest keeping it on the quiet side. We don't want my aunt out here witnessing the pain and torture."

"Don't worry. Lulu isn't going to make much noise. She can't have anyone witnessing her humiliation. Where shall I take the prisoner, sir?"

"Don't care. No longer interested. You take care of the problem for me, Mink and Dirk."

Kit found herself pulled away from the wall toward the stairs. "Hey," she said. "Where...are we going? I'm not...dressed!"

Her protest brought those hypnotic eyes to her body. The night was warm and she was wearing her camisole and matching panties.

"Me neither," Lucas said. "Dare ya to come along. I promise to be the perfect gentleman."

"You aren't leaving me here with Mink and Dirk!" Lulu protested. "Mink, you let go right now or I swear I'll hurt you the moment I'm free."

"I want to hear pleas of mercy, not threats, from my prisoner," the guy on top of Lulu said, a big smile still on his face.

The man—Mink?—seemed to be having a lot of fun, but maybe she should come to her friend's aid. Kit tried to shake her hand loose. "I should help Lulu. Besides, I don't even know you."

"If you know my sister, she has a black belt and can take on Mink."

"Ha, I would but I don't want to break any bones!" Lulu said.

"You see, that doesn't help your situation at all," Mink said. "Next you'll threaten to kill me and then where would that leave us? I'd have no option but to tie you up and do bad things to you. Hey, got some rope, Dirk?"

"I'm out of here," the man by the stairs said. "Third wheel and all that. Things look pretty much in control here."

Third wheel, what? She wanted to get out of there too and just forget about the whole thing. It was bad enough to be caught by Miss Clementine out here with "improper attire" on. She was sure it would be mentioned to her mother and then her father would hear about it. That was all she needed, another long talk with her already paranoid parents.

"Hey, uh, no," Kit interrupted. "I...I really think we should all just go to bed. Oh shit. I didn't mean that! Not that way!"

Her face felt as if it was on fire as all three men started laughing. Even Lulu was cracking up.

Lucas scratched his chin. "What way?"

Kit sniffed. She looked down pointedly at her hand still in his. "You can let go now."

"What if you jump on my back again and pull my chest hair?"

Lulu snickered. "Next time, Kit, pull some out."

Kit rolled her eyes. Her hand felt strangely cold after having been in his warm grasp. "Okay, getting in the middle of sibling fights was obviously a mistake. Bad habit from having my own pack of brothers. Lulu, I so wanted to help you, but you look quite...happy...right now. So I'm off. Really, I've got to get some rest because we're moving furniture tomorrow bright and early, remember?"

That was why she was here, to help Lulu out. Miss Clementine was getting up in years and had decided to leave her favorite niece the B&B as her inheritance. Lulu was super-excited because she had loved the old restored mansion and her aunt was going to show her the ropes of running a B&B. Kit was excited for Lulu too. Her friend had a great deal of talent at management and creative decoration, and a B&B like this would be perfect for someone who loved to micro-manage as much as Lulu.

"Hey, don't leave me with them!" Lulu pleaded now. "You heard their threats. They're going to dangle me off the rails! Mink, if you don't let me up, I swear I'm going to post that pic all over the place and then you'll be sorry."

"Ha, I think this one needs more convincing she's no longer in control, Sir!" Mink said.

"And stop addressing my brother and asking permission for everything! I'm going to—"

"You have my permission to torture her," Cucumber interrupted. "Of course, leave no marks and make sure she can still carry some furniture in the morning."

"Aye, sir!" Mink got to his feet, hauling Lulu up in one swift motion and pulling her toward another door. "Come on, you and I are going to work out your form of punishment unless you give me that camera."

Lulu kicked out. Mink jumped back. Lulu opened the door to her room and ran in. Mink dived through it before the heavy door closed with a thud. Silence.

Kit coughed. "Umm. My brother would never allow another guy to manhandle me like that."

"Have you ever taken a picture of your brother in The Pink Room?"

Kit's eyes widened. Lulu put three SEALs in The Pink Room? She couldn't help herself. She grinned. "Nope. But now I'm going to have to."

"If you did, would he retaliate?"

She nodded. "Yeah, but he wouldn't send two of his friends after her."

"Hey, I'm not in there," Dirk interrupted. "In fact, I think I'm going to head off to The Pink Room to stare at some pink cherubs."

Lucas was looking at Kit so intently she was starting to feel uncomfortable. "I think you should go too," she said softly.

"I'm giving Mink five minutes," Lucas stated, just as softly.

Kit rolled her eyes. "I hope Lulu is kicking his ass."

Lucas' slow smile made her feel hot and cold at the same time. He leaned one big shoulder against the wall.

"Let's not talk about my sister and Mink behind that door," he said. "What's your name and I like your nightie very much."

Kit had worn less at the pool but this man's hot gaze made her feel totally exposed. He was too close, and knowing how hard his body was against hers added to the odd tension in the air.

She stuck out her hand, trying to make things normal. "I'm Kit, a friend of Lulu's. It's actually Kit-Ling but most people call me Kit." She chose to ignore his second remark about her clothing. "And you're Lucas, the brother."

He took her hand but he didn't shake it. "Kit-Ling. I like that. *Moi malenkei kotonok.*" His smile was slow and devastating. "Very fitting."

"Huh? Moi what?" Kit frowned. It must be the late hour that was making her do dumb things because she had just given him her hand again. "What did you just say?"

He gave a small shake of his head. "Not telling you till you agree to go out with me."

She swallowed. "You're quick."

"I could be quicker, if you like. But mind you, we're still outside my aunt's door." He squeezed her hand gently. "Mink will be coming out soon. Give me an answer."

"Hey, a girl needs to think about these things. We've just met."

"You climbed my back. I like the feel of your...you...against me. Let's kiss and see how we like that."

She stared at him, then narrowed her eyes. Boy, the man had a one-track mind, didn't he? "You went from asking me for a date to a kiss. Not very subtle, are you?"

He shook his head again. "Subtle doesn't work in life. At this moment, the way you look, subtle is the last thing on my mind." He took a step closer, a gleam in his dark eyes "What do you say, a kiss, and if you like it, a date? I bet you're going to like both. Very much."

She cocked her head. Confident devil. She liked the way his eyes crinkled when he smiled. Correction. Confident *and* handsome devil. "My brother has a name for SEALs like you. He's Airborne, you know."

Lucas flashed her a wicked grin. "My sister calls me names too. Do you think I'd worry about what an Airborne cupcake calls a SEAL?"

She raised her eyebrows. "Ooooh. Nice. Airborne Cupcake. I've got to remember to use that *and* tell him who passed on that nickname to me. I'll bet he'd want to make you his cupcake, then."

"Nah, not into pissing contests." His voice lowered. "I'd rather be your cupcake. Come on, take a bite."

It was so awfully tempting. Kit knew a lot about SEALs, having interviewed and talked to them in her job. Being a public information associate for a web-based broadcasting service had its perks. But her interaction had never been this up close and personal, and in the present surroundings, in her current state of undress, it was very difficult to pretend to be professional.

She stood on her tippy-toes.

And bit him on the lower lip gently.

He pulled her closer and his lips caught hers. Her free hand came up against the rock cliff that was his chest. She felt his free hand on the small of her back. She opened her mouth in protest. His tongue delved in. And in a split second, there was no space between them. Like she'd said, he was damn quick.

* * *

Lucas was never one to wait too long about anything. His lifestyle didn't promote that kind of philosophy. Live for the moment. Do it now; you might not have a second chance. Enjoy the things a man should enjoy—pretty women, good food, simple things.

People might say that was a really shallow way to live. Well, yeah, tote an AK-47 and fifty pounds of ammo up and down mountain terrain or run through the desert on one can of water while going after people who shoot back, asshole. Then come talk to him about simple things and shallow living.

Normally, cupcakes weren't his style. For one thing, they were often too small and sweet and gone in one bite. But damn if this particular cupcake didn't taste fine. She wasn't too small for just one taste either. She fitted his body fine too. He could think of a dozen naughty ways of fitting inside her and sinking his teeth into this delectable morsel.

She was kissing him back boldly. He liked that. In fact, he liked a lot about this woman so far. She had a saucy tongue and the way she'd joined in to help Lulu suggested someone who didn't think too much before jumping into the fray of things. If that was true, the next couple of days looked very promising indeed.

He slid her hand down his chest, enjoying the feel of her nails scraping lightly across his skin. She made a sound in her throat and snuggled closer. He explored the curve of her back and moved lower. She arched against him. Oh yeah.

The sound of a door opening interrupted his amorous line of thought.

Damn, damn, damn. Not Aunt Clementine again.

"Ahem." It was Mink. Then, a little louder, "ahem, ahem."

With great reluctance, Lucas lifted his head. "I heard you the first time," he said.

"Sorry," Mink said, "but Lulu is coming out in a sec and I thought you'd better not tempt her to take another photo with her camera."

Lucas cocked a brow. "Is the mission accomplished?"

"Oh, yeah. Deleted. Rechecked. And the perp properly punished." Mink grinned his trademark flash of a smile, teeth white against his tan. "Very properly."

Hmm. The few times they'd been together, he'd noticed Mink showing signs toward his sister. "I see," Lucas said. "I hope you didn't cross the line. You are, after all, in your underwear and were in a room with my sister."

"I'm still in my underwear, aren't I?" Mink pointed out solicitously.

A tap on his shoulder. Lucas looked down. "Yes, Cupcake?"

She frowned. "No, that's what you are, remember?" She reminded him politely. "You're the cupcake and I was invited to bite you."

Oh yeah. He ignored Mink's smirk. He had to remember the woman had a brother and probably knew many insidious ways to get back at men. And that brought back Mink's warning. Lulu. He let go of Kit reluctantly.

"I'm doing this under duress," he told her in a soft voice. "Another time, I'd insist on a bigger bite."

Her face had a pretty flush, even though she rolled her eyes. Before she could answer, the door behind Mink opened and Lulu came out, looking defiant as she gathered her hair into a ponytail.

Lucas turned, crossed his arms and gave her his best big brother look. "Are we done playing?" he asked. "Because you know you've lost this one."

"Oh, I'll get another chance," Lulu said airily. She gestured to Kit. "Come along. We have things to discuss."

"Umm. Can I just go to sleep?" Kit asked, in a hopeful voice. "It *is* pretty late."

"Traitor."

Kit put up her hands in surrender. "Okay. Nighty-night. Not going to stand out here all night."

"Yeah, you're keeping Aunt Clementine awake," Lucas chimed in.

His sister took the bait. "Oh no, you're not making me out to be the bad guy, brother. This was for what you did the last time and I'm going to tell Aunty Clementine all about it."

Lucas grinned. The seeds of future vengeance had been planted. He turned to Kit. "Goodnight," he said, letting his gaze do the talking.

He couldn't see the exact shade, but her eyes were a pretty lighter color. There was amusement in them and then she winked, as if she knew what he was up to.

"'Night."

He sent Mink a look and they started down the stairs. Behind him, the girls were speaking softly.

"Traitor," his sister reiterated, although she didn't sound indignant. "You sided with my horrid frog brother."

"Aw, he's a cupcake."

Lucas' grin widened. He was already hungry for breakfast. But first things first. The moment they were out of hearing, he casually asked, "Now, what did you do to my sister again?"

Mink scratched the back of his neck. That was usually a sign that he was skipping a few things in his story.

"I tackled her and snagged the camera. Then I sat on her while I deleted the photo."

Lucas glanced at his friend briefly. "You know my sister can take down a man twice your size, right?"

Mink shrugged. "I sat on her hard."

They reached the Pink Room. Lucas turned to Mink.

"I know she's a grown-up now, but I feel obliged to give you that big brother warning, you know? Don't mess with my sister's feelings, man."

Mink shook his head. He turned the door knob. "Hey, I'm taking it as slow as she wants, dude."

Lucas put out a hand, stopping the door from opening wider. "Gotcha," he said. "You *have* been messing around with my sister."

Mink shrugged. "Your sister is a fine woman and I wouldn't just mess around with her." The light streaming out of the Pink Room caught the gleam in his eyes. "Is that the right answer?"

"Hey, you two having a secret pow-wow outside the door or what?" Dirk called out. "It's freaking cold on this fucking giant bed without you two to cuddle next to. And the pink's slowly killing me here."

Lucas shook his head and let go of the door. "God help me and all lonely SEALs," he said as he walked in. "Can we turn off the lights and get some shut eye now? Then we won't see the pink till morning."

"Sure, you two had your fun and I'm the lonely stooge cuddling up to the cherubs in here," Dirk complained in a mournful voice.

"We'll find you a real angel," Mink promised.

"Lights out," Lucas ordered.

"Hey, Cuke," Mink said, in the darkness.

Lucas gave a loud sigh. He had hoped for some reprieve. But these were his buddies and he knew what was coming.

"Cupcake is a cutie," Mink said.

"Cupcake?" Dirk asked.

"Yeah, he called her Cupcake."

"Cucumber and Cupcake. Sounds like a fucking tea party."

Ignoring the male chuckles, Lucas closed his eyes and stretched. Life was either hell or a party. Either way, he always had his best friends with him.

CHAPTER TWO

It was just a kiss. A very nice one, with a very hot-looking guy. That was all.

Kit tried to put it out of her mind as she got ready the next morning, but it was tough when Lulu kept teasing her about last night.

"So, what do you think of my brother?" She asked.

"Big dude. Moving furniture should be a piece of cake," Kit answered, keeping her voice level.

"Uh-huh. He's single and as far as I know, has no girlfriend. And you're single too. Lucas is much better than that clueless guy you dated a month ago."

Lord. The Bransons did not skirt around a topic.

Kit stuck out her tongue. "Are you trying to set me up with your brother now?"

"Hey, I've been trying to give him away since forever. Want him?"

"No, thanks. I have my own big brother to fight with."

"Yeah, you two were fighting last night." Lulu laughed as she ducked the pillow Kit threw at her.

Breakfast was going to be a noisy affair. Aunt Clementine kept everything very informal and the guests usually showed up between 7am and 10am for a buffet style Continental breakfast which was included with their stay. With five extra mouths, though, Kit and Lulu came down early to help in the kitchen, but Mrs. Talbot, the longtime cook, had everything under control. All they needed to do was set the tables outside and make sure there was enough fresh coffee made.

"My brother loves coffee. A dash of cream," Lulu told her, as they moved around the tables in the dining room.

"And you're giving me this tidbit of information why?" Kit asked, as she placed the cups on the serving platter.

"For your file, you know, the one you're keeping for your project about military men."

Kit snorted. "You're just jealous I'm going off to spend some time researching about military stuff."

"Oh, is that what we're calling it now?" Lulu mocked, putting the vase of fresh cut flowers by the window.

Although she aimed for informal, Miss Clementine wanted an Old World feel, so there were no plastic platters or containers, no paper napkins, nothing that "looked too modern." The only concession she'd made were the very modern coffee pots sitting on the hot plates, but even those had pretty pink dollies underneath them.

Kit grinned. Miss Clementine must love pink.

Sounds of male voices carried down the corridor into the dining area. Even from here, she could guess to whom they belonged. They came in, looking disgustingly male—clean shaven, hair slicked back, alert eyes taking in their surroundings.

She studied the tallest of them surreptitiously. Okay, it was tough to be surreptitious when the specimen was at least six foot three and was standing only a few feet away. He was just as impressive-looking in daylight. Dark-haired, strong-jawed, tee shirt stretched to display broad chest, muscular arms and a narrow waist, followed by those memorable long legs in fitted jeans. It wasn't just the good looks, but the whole impact of his absolute maleness—in his prime, strong, dominant. One couldn't help but stare at the darn man. Nobody should look this delicious. Especially for breakfast.

To her chagrin—and secret delight—Lucas Branson was looking straight at her, with that unsettling intent-filled gaze from the night before. She made herself look busy, turning nonchalantly to Lulu to ask a question, but her girlfriend, it seemed, had eyes only for that other SEAL, Mink.

"Lulu," Kit said. "Where are the smaller plates?"

Lulu blinked. "Oh. Umm, yeah. Let me get them." She hurried off, leaving Kit alone with three hungry guys.

"Good morning," Lucas greeted, a slow smile forming. "How was your night?"

"Good," Kit replied. "Breakfast is buffet-style, so just get whatever you need, boys. Miss Clementine had an extra batch made just for you all. She said she knows how much you eat."

Lucas sniffed the air appreciatively. "Yeah. We tend to eat a lot. Are you joining us?"

"In a bit."

"Good. You look nice in pants too, even though I prefer last night's outfit."

Not as nice as he looked in shorts. "Don't you ever stop flirting?" Kit asked, handing him a plate from the stack.

"I don't flirt. I just state it like it is. Don't I, boys?"

"Yeah," Dirk agreed, as he scooped scrambled eggs onto his plate. "Lucas is all about statements."

"Lucas' statements are like bumper stickers," Mink said, blowing on his coffee. "Every statement has style."

Kit sniffed. "Did you take a shower? You two are full of it already and it's still early."

"Hey, now, we smell good!" Dirk sniffed at his shoulder. "Mink squirted me with some pink...what was that stuff you sprayed on me, bro?"

"French toilet water," Mink said helpfully. "Pink French toilet water."

The two of them laughed.

"Be careful, boys, she has Ranger brothers," Lulu said, as she came in, arms loaded down with plates.

Mink got up and went to help her. "Yeah, we heard. That's why your friend keeps sniffing so suspiciously. Rangers are notoriously smelly."

Kit grinned. She was going to have some great lines for her brother when he got home. "No wonder he calls you guys cupcakes. Afraid of a little dirt."

"What? I'll have you know..."

"Remind me to let you smell my..."

"I'll show him my cupcakes..."

The men all protested together after that and Lulu and she exchanged grins as they rolled their eyes.

"So easy," Lulu mouthed. Aloud, she said, "Aunty Clementine said to join in and eat, Kit. Everything's been taken care of already."

Kit went to serve herself. Honestly, this place ran like clockwork and there wasn't much she could do to help out. The hard work would come when they started moving the furniture. Lucas pulled out a chair across from where he was seated.

"Thank you," she said. "How's breakfast?"

"Good," He helped scoot her chair in, leaned down and continued, "I like the tattoo on your lower back. How did you get it and what do you do for fun?"

His tone was low and intimate. It made her heart go pitter-patter. There was no polite back-and-forth inane conversation with this guy. "You know, there's such a thing as social niceties," she said and secretly grimaced at how prim she sounded.

"48 hours don't allow for social niceties." He leaned closer. "I want to get to know you better. That's being nice, right?"

Kit spooned sugar into her coffee. "Nope. I call that rude. Desperate, even. Are you a desperate man, Lucas?"

"Sometimes." He went back to his seat. "But I'm not there yet."

She studied him as she took a sip. He gazed back at her, a serious expression betrayed only by the tiny quirk of his lips. Most women would find that directness very unsettling, but it was a refreshing change for her. Her job required her to use words carefully, to interpret what others meant when they said things a certain way. There were no such games with this man.

"Forty-eight hours?" she asked. "I thought you were in town for three days." Lulu had supplied that piece of information.

The small quirk of his lips was now an amused curve. "It was my secret weapon. I was keeping the third day for desperate measures."

She laughed and took a bite of her bagel. "Or maybe you'd be resting up, tired out by all the moving."

His smile widened even more. He had beautiful straight teeth. "It depends on how much moving we do."

Gulp.

Thankfully, Lulu appeared with a tray and sat next to her. She deposited some toast onto her brother's plate, then turned to Kim.

"The trick is to keep his mouth occupied at all times. Then he can't bother you with inane conversation."

"You know, Mink tells me the same thing about you," Lucas said.

Mink was drinking his coffee and started choking. Dirk helpfully thumped his back. Lulu tossed all three of them a glare, daring them to continue the conversation, but Lucas just ignored her, catching Kit's amused gaze with his. Laughter lines crinkled the corner of his eyes, betraying his enjoyment of his sister's discomfiture.

"Do you have the same problem with my sister, Kit?" he continued. "Yak, yak, yak, yak, yak."

Lulu reached over and smacked his arm. Just then a couple of guests came into the dining room.

"Good morning!" one of them greeted.

There was a chorus of 'good mornings' and everyone settled back to eating. Kit breathed out a sigh. It wouldn't have been good if the regular guests had come in a few seconds later in a middle of a sibling food fight.

As if reading her mind, Lucas said, in a low voice, "Don't worry. We really know how to behave."

Lulu snorted and whispered, "Yeah, like Kit's going to believe you after last night." She smiled at the guests. "Make yourselves comfortable. Sit anywhere you want."

From then on, the boys were on their best behavior, charming two older women in their sixties who came and sat by them, asking them questions and joking with them about going out dancing.

Kit listened quietly, enjoying the friendly camaraderie and thinking about her job. Her request to broaden her public information role to include some field reporting had been approved and she was excited about the next meeting with the board so she could listen in on the plans for the next few projects. It would be great if she could work with Sean Castro and his ongoing assignment.

"You seem far away," Lulu said, interrupting her reverie. "Planning your next reports?"

Kit shook her head. "I finished those before coming. Don't want to do homework when I'm on vacay!"

Lulu smiled. "You consider helping me move a holiday?"

"Hey, good company, good food and hopefully, a night out with my girlfriend—that's vacation, right?"

"True." Lulu buttered her toast. "Once the boys move the heavy stuff, I can take care of the rest. We'll go out then, 'kay?"

"Yeah."

"Hey, what about us?" Mink chimed in. "Don't we get to have a night off?"

"Are you angling to be part of our girls' night out, pack mule?" Lulu asked.

"Did you hear that? We're nothing but pack mules," Mink said.

"I think she's calling you an ass, dude," Dirk said.

"Maybe because she got her ass kicked last night," Mink pointed out.

"What?"

Oh, oh. It'd started again. Kit looked across the table at Lucas. Her pulse raced into a gallop. He was watching her, totally ignoring his friends and sister. Everything around them seemed to recede into the background.

It's just a look, Kit.

She wasn't a shy person, never considered herself special in any particular way, but that look. Oh God. Focused. Intimate. Her insides churned and melted from the heat in his eyes. It made her feel very shy. And special.

This close, she could see his eyes weren't brown or black, like she'd assumed. They were dark gray. The color of his tee shirt brought out hints of blue in them. Every time they settled on her, she was compelled to look back, wanting to know more about this man's secret thoughts.

That made her want to laugh out loud. Lulu would tell her that men, and especially her brother, had no secret thoughts. She'd often scoffed at how easy it was to read men. Kit didn't explain to her friend it was so for her because she was leggy, curvaceous and model-gorgeous. Lulu had this self-image that she was a regular tomboy and that was part of the fun of being her friend, watching Lulu wonder what was up with all these guys talking like nervous teenagers around her.

"Hey, Cumber, you didn't answer. Are we doing anything as exciting?"

His eyes never left hers. "I'm making plans."

"Umm, do they include us?" Dirk asked wryly.

"Maybe. Depends."

Kit glanced down at her food. Food. Her light-headedness must be from the lack of food.

"You aren't planning anything until you get to work," Lulu interrupted her steamy thoughts. "And pack mules don't get lunch if they don't get started soon. Go on, shoo. Get the van unloaded."

"Can I finish my coffee first?"

"Tough woman, man."

"I think she just needs someone else to push around so we're left in peace."

"You volunteering, Mink?"

"Oh, sure, suddenly I'm relegated to become a target."

"No, target is lunch, dude. You're just distraction fodder. With Cumber's permission, of course. Right, Cumber?"

"Humph. I'm getting tired of this asking for permission stuff," Lulu interrupted the men's banter. "I'll be in the back, unloading, when you guys are ready. You coming soon, Kit?"

Kit took a quick swallow of the rest of her juice and got up. She snapped a salute. "Oh yes, right now, ma'am."

Escape seemed like a good idea. Let the boys eat and then she'd deal with Lucas Branson later.

"See you guys later," Kit said.

She deliberately didn't glance at Lucas' direction as she followed Lulu out, but felt his eyes on her all the way. She stopped to get an apple off the buffet table.

"Target escaping, dude," she heard Dirk mocking Mink. "You should be the first to go help out the lady. You know she's expecting you to run after her."

"I'm playing hard to get," Mink said. "Hey, Cumber, pass me the salt."

Kit grinned to herself. Luckily, Lulu was out of hearing distance.

"What do you say, Cumber? Let the girls decide what stuff to move around first or go out and take over the whole operation?"

"Let's wait a few minutes," she heard Lucas say as she headed out. "I'm enjoying the view from here."

CHAPTER THREE

Two nights later

"That woman is an organized taskmaster, dude!" Dirk said, giving the waitress a smile as she put the mugs of beer in front of them.

"She'd make a good sergeant," Lucas agreed. He took a long gulp of the frothy brew. "Ahhhhh. Been wanting that all day."

They had moved Lulu's furniture into her suite of rooms the first day. Tricky business, maneuvering beds and desks up and down curvy wooden staircases. Getting the old furniture down from the upper rooms took a bit of brain and muscle. They had bought some tough ropes to lower some of the pieces over the banister. The heavier oak was a slower process, requiring a fair amount of quiet cussing.

After that, it was bringing up Lulu's stuff. They had to disassemble her big work desk and part of her bed so it would fit through one of the smaller doorways. There were a couple of bookshelves and what seemed like five million boxes of books and clothes.

"How did they do all that moving in the old days, anyway?" Mink asked. "I know they had servants but that old oak furniture we moved down was massive and damn heavy. The girls would never have been able to do that themselves."

When the truck which was supposed to pick up the older stuff for some charity didn't show up, they had to move all the furniture from the curb to the back shed in the evening. Not a problem for the guys but the delay had caused extra work.

Dirk flexed a bicep and pointed to it. "Muscles. Just like the way we did it."

"I bet they needed more than three men. We got Cumber. He's worth at least two in strength."

Lucas lifted a brow.

"Okay, three," Dirk amended.

"Better," Lucas said, amused.

"I don't know, dude. 'Men were like real men back during the *wahr*,'" Mink said, affecting Aunt Clementine's soft Southern accent so accurately, it made them laugh.

Aunt Clementine had been something else. She was determined to "chaperone" the girls as much as she could and was constantly telling them tales from 'back during the *wahr*.' Lucas was never sure whether she'd meant the Civil War or the World Wars, but one thing was for sure, 'during the *wahr*,' men had been stronger than any today, more handsome, more courteous, more manly. Her aunt's voice was dreamy when she had talked about her first love and how he'd courted her, and afterward, Lucas and the Stooges had jokingly wondered whether this lover was also from the Civil War.

"Well, what do you expect in Charleston? Many women I meet here have this thing about the Civil War. And then they look at me and don't see Rhett Butler," Mink said, putting two straws in his nose to make a mustache and then added, "Frankly, my dear, I don't give a...gosh be-darn."

"You are such an ass. Do you think Miss Clementine sees us as men?" Dirk asked.

"I'm sure she knows we go out and fight in wars," Cumber said, "but I think she romanticizes the Civil War and sort of gets them all mixed up in her head. I'd imagine it gets like that when you have to tell the same Civil War history stuff about the mansion to your guests every day."

"Man, I sure hope your sis doesn't get to be like that when she runs the place," Mink said. "Don't want her to get those kinds of romantic notions about men and war."

Lucas squinted his eyes at his friend who was still fiddling with his Rhett Butler imitation mustache, half-amused at the way he was trying to cut the straws with his pen-knife to the right length to fit above his lip. "Speaking of romantic notions and my sister, what kind are you contemplating with Lulu?"

Mink and Lulu. He'd had suspicions for a while now but these last couple of days had confirmed it. Mink had his eyes on his sister, and surprisingly, she didn't seem to mind. He'd never thought about his sister being interested in his best friends and wasn't sure how to deal with it.

"Oh-oh," Dirk said and held up his mug. "Should I leave the table for this private brother to brother-in-arms warning?"

"Nah. I'm just asking," Lucas said. "Well?"

Mink looked down at his beer. "Well, nothing. You know what I think about romantic notions. They're for women. No offense, man. Your sister and I are just flirting, nothing more. She has a mansion to take care of and I have battles to fight."

"Hey, sounds like a Civil War story to me," Dirk quipped, then waved his mug at Mink. "Hey, joking here, Rhett."

"Just don't hurt my sister's feelings," Lucas said. "I don't want none of that big brother must beat the shit out of his best friend crap in the future, you hear?"

"I think your sister can beat the crap out of me without your help, Cumber," Mink pointed out dryly. He put on his straw "mustache" again. This time, they fit perfectly. "Scarlett O'Hara she ain't."

That was true. Lucas signaled to the waitress for another round. "Fine. Subject closed."

"Oh, no, you don't. Romantic notions, baby. How about Miss Kit there, big fella? We see you doing more than making eyes with her the last two days." Dirk batted his eyes and affected Aunt Clementine's accent too as he added, "Lucas, can you come back here and help Kit carry this? Oh, yes, Lucas, it's such a beautiful evening, go take Kit for a walk."

Mink snickered.

Lucas grinned. Kit was something else too. She'd found ways to slip from Aunt Clementine by putting the ideas into the older woman's head. Dirk was exaggerating but he didn't mind the teasing. He'd enjoyed the moments alone with Kit.

He looked behind Dirk and saw Lulu and Kit coming to their table. He made a small signal to his buddies.

"Well, well, if it isn't the three stooges," Lulu said. She turned and stared hard at Mink, who still had the shortened straws sticking out his nose. "What in the world is that above your lip?"

"My Rhett Butler mustache," Mink said.

Kit laughed out loud. Lucas got up to bring a couple of extra chairs over.

"That looks disgusting. They wiggle when you speak."

Mink half-closed his eyes. "I'll have you know, Rhett Butler was considered dashing, sexy, manly, masterful, confident..."

"Arrogant, roguish, insufferable..." chimed in Lulu.

"Oy, adjectives give me a headache. I need more beer!" Dirk interrupted.

On cue, the waitress appeared with a tray of mugs. She deposited them and turned to get the women's orders.

Mink nudged Lucas. "Notions tonight, yes?"

Lucas gave Mink a long look. "I don't want to hear about your notions if it involved you-know-who, clear?"

"Aye, aye, sir!"

"But we want details on yours."

Ignoring his two friends' meaningful smirks, Lucas picked up his beer and turned to Kit. "It's our last night together. Let's do something memorable."

She had on a pretty long-sleeved top with swirly patterns. And her hair fell in waves around her shoulders.

He wanted to take her outside and be with her alone. He knew his friends wouldn't mind, but his sister might, seeing that it was their "girls night out," as they called it.

"I think these last few days have been pretty memorable," Kit said, with a slight smile. She folded her thumb and fingers as she counted. "The Pink Room and imagining all three of you in that bed, Mink in his underwear, Dirk hanging off the balustrade, you carrying that huge armoire with that lampshade on your head, Miss Clementine's shocked face when she caught you boys wearing the beads and laces, and now Mink with his Rhett Butler mustache."

Her chuckles were infectious and they all joined in.

"Hey, it was Lulu who put the lampshade on Cumber's head. He couldn't do a thing because he had his arms full of that damn oak tree."

"It's an armoire," Lulu corrected. "And he looked very nice wearing a lampshade."

"And so did a dozen of your friends, seeing that you posted that picture online," Lucas said wryly.

Lulu grinned. "I wish it was the first picture, in the pink bed with them." She looked at Mink and Dirk. "Now, that would have been soooooo funny. Ah well, the pink lampshade will have to do."

Lucas wagged a finger at her. "Payback is a bitch, sis," he threatened softly. He put his hand on the back of Kit's chair and noted her stiffening ever so slightly, betraying her awareness of him. "But not tonight. I'm in a good mood and not going to let you spoil it."

He had enjoyed himself these few days. Downtime with family was rare and he savored every moment. His job as a SEAL was a demanding and dangerous one. Each operation abroad could be the last one, so he tried to see his folks every chance he got.

This time, he'd managed a lunch with his parents before heading to Charleston to help Lulu. Plus, he'd met Kit, someone he would like to see again, and hopefully, vice-versa. Family, friends, and meeting Kit. All in all, a damn good visit home.

"What did you have for dinner?" Kit asked. "Lulu took us to a seafood place."

Lucas shrugged. "Meat and potatoes. Then we wandered around King St. and hung out at a couple of dive bars. Drank some at the Upper Deck. Ended up here because we can talk and have snacks."

"Lulu said you guys would be in this bar."

Lucas smiled. "You looking for me?"

She had a really sweet smile, with a big dimple on one side. "Yes. But only because you're such a cupcake."

He leaned over and put his mouth against her ear. "Want another bite?"

"More than one, please," she said.

Lucas' smile widened. She was his kind of woman.

* * *

Kit couldn't believe it. Usually, it didn't take long for the investigative reporter in her to figure the whys and wherefores she liked or disliked anyone, especially a man. It was in her nature to listen and probe, to analyze and make connections with their stories. But somehow, in the last three days, Lucas Branson had disconnected that little bit of wiring in her head.

She'd done completely un-Kit-like things. Her brother had warned her about spec ops. operatives on leave, that they were coming down from a high and were sometimes looking for a good time before returning to the field. Heck, her brother exemplified that behavior constantly with his many female acquaintances. Being the snoop she was, she'd once stolen his little black book (she'd rolled her eyes at the whole cliché of it all—a little black book, seriously?) and thumbed through all the female names and phone numbers. She'd even considered playing a mean joke and calling all of them to meet "him" at the same place but had thought better of it. She had, however, led him to believe she did.

She still grinned at the memory of the horrified expression stuck on his face. Oh, brotherly rage was always a fine sight.

Being brought up in a household of protective males had its setbacks too, of course. Her dates were often intimidated to the point of never staying around too long. Her father alone had scared away most of them, but then her brothers all grew up and a couple of them had followed her dad into the army and geez, dating life, bye-bye. She loved her family to pieces and understood they had her best interest at heart, but life with overbearing men could drive one crazy after a while.

That was why she really enjoyed her friendship with Lulu, who had the same type of family. However, her pal was also an Amazon Queen who took charge of her life. Her father and brother, from what Kit could see, gave her room.

Kit studied Lucas, who was, at that moment, bantering with his sister. On one hand, he was exactly like a big brother to Lulu; on the other hand, not once had he intruded on his sister's privacy by asking her about Mink. She thought of the other night when Mink had been in the room alone with Lulu. *In his underwear.* Her own brother would've torn down that door. Yet, Lucas had just waited outside. Sure, there was brotherly protectiveness there but there was also trust that his friend wouldn't go too far.

She had been intrigued. Was still intrigued.

"I'd rather not hang out here all night," Lucas said, turning to her. "What do you want to do?"

She glanced over at Lulu, who shrugged. "I'm game for anything. What do you have in mind?"

"Some alone time." He stood up and offered her his hand. "We can all meet back here later. Mink and Dirk, you're not to let Lulu out of your sight."

"What?" Lulu protested. "You're leaving me with them and kidnapping my friend?"

"Only for a little while. Here, go see a movie. The guys are funny at the movies."

"You suck!" Lulu said while snatching the money Lucas threw on the table. "Bribery doesn't work with little sister anymore!"

Kit laughed because Lulu loved going to the movies. This was the classic big brother bribe.

"And babysitters should be paid too!" Mink chimed in. "I mean, the girl needs two babysitters. Right, Dirk?"

The two SEALs high-fived each other.

"You okay with this?" Kit asked Lulu.

Her friend smiled and waved her away. "I know how to get into trouble on my own," she said, then winked. "Besides, who wants her brother along when she has two SEALs to play with?"

Kit grinned. True.

"Okay, we meet back here later. Text us when the movie is over," Lucas ordered. "And don't get my men in trouble, Lulu. We're due back on duty first thing and I can't break them out of jail."

Lulu snorted and gave Kit another wave before turning to Mink and Dirk. "Boys," she said in silky tones, "I'm in the mood for a romantic comedy."

Lucas shook his head and gestured to Kit to exit the noisy scene, made more so by the howls of protests from the two SEALs at the table. She grabbed her jacket and purse and walked with him out of the bar.

The night air was cool and felt good after being in a crowded place, so she didn't put on her jacket. They climbed down the steps and headed away from the lights and noise. She had no idea where he was taking her but figured it would be somewhere quiet and a little more private. She hoped so, anyway.

It was the last night she was going to see this man. Not forever, perhaps, but other than the fact that they shared a mutual attraction, she had no idea what was ahead. Did he want to see her again? Why was she even thinking about this when she should be concentrating on her new career plans? For all she knew, she was just a passing fancy, someone to flirt with while he was in town. Too many questions. Why was she always asking so many questions when she should be enjoying this moment, this man?

"Looking forward to getting back to work?" she asked, to break the silence.

"Why do you say that? Trying to get rid of me already?"

His tone was light but she couldn't be sure in the semi-darkness.

"Well, moving furniture around can't be as exciting as toting machine guns and taking down enemies," she said.

"Sometimes boring stuff to normal people can be interesting and exciting to those of us who live a pretty rigid lifestyle," he told her. "We get to appreciate little things as meaningful and important."

He squeezed her hand. It felt natural, walking with him like this, with the cool breeze from the river blowing against her face, and the lights from the bridge twinkling not far away.

"So, what meaningful thing did you get from moving furniture?" She was curious how he viewed things in general. In her experience, from watching her family and interviewing returning military personnel, they were, more often than not, unable to function normally for a while.

"I met you."

His swift reply brought a smile to her lips. Military men also flirted a lot.

"Okay, besides that."

There was a short pause. "I'm not good at explaining things," he finally said, adding, with some ruefulness, "at least, without using a lot of curse words. I try not to do that back home so much but when I talk too long, they slip out sometimes."

"My brother is..."

"...a fucking Airborne Ranger," he finished for her and laughed quietly. "You keep saying that like a shield."

Surprise stopped her in mid-stride and she stumbled, since he'd kept on walking. His arms came around her, pulling her close. His scent—a mixture of maleness, leather and cologne—played with her senses.

"A shield?" She repeated. "That's ridiculous. I was just trying to explain I'm used to hearing bad language around me. Believe me, my brothers don't censor much."

"Mmmhmm."

He didn't seem interested in whatever she was saying at the moment and she shivered a little when his hands slid up her hips and under her sweater. His warm hands caressed her lower back as he pulled her close.

"Lucas," she began. "There are people around us."

Not that many, but still. She was kind of afraid if he started kissing her, she was going to embarrass herself by climbing all over him. The revelation of how strong her attraction for him was both startled and unnerved her.

"Yeah, and then someone you know would probably take a picture of us, plaster it all over some social media and then your Ranger brother will show up on my ship demanding to defend his little sister's honor," he mocked. "Quaking in my boots here."

She giggled at the thought. "That was a mighty long sentence and not one cuss word," she mocked back.

His hands traveled higher, molding her body against his. "They're all in my head right now," he said huskily. "Pages and pages filled with words like fuck and tongue and...my something something inside your something something. Lady, you don't know how hard I am right now."

His self-censorship made her burst out in laughter. Recklessly, she reached up and grabbed him by the collar with both hands, pulling his head lower.

"Show me," she invited. "Let's get a room and show me those pages and pages."

"Who's being quick now?" he teased.

"You did ask for a memorable night," she told him.

He bent his head lower. Just as she'd known, the moment his lips touched hers, it felt as if she was one of those fireworks being set off. She responded fiercely, unthinkingly. His tongue slid against her, invading like silky honey. She felt the sexual heat snaking its way down her whole being. She hardly knew this man, but she knew she desired him with a burning intensity. She snuggled against him, wanting more.

"Get a room!" A passing stranger yelled out in an amused voice.

Kit laid her forehead against his chest when he released her lips. Her ears were buzzing, her lips felt swollen, and her heart was doing gymnastic tricks. She knew it. She knew she would forget where she was once that gorgeous mouth met hers. Anticipation had only fueled her passion.

"Yeah, I think we will," Lucas agreed in a low, sexy voice.

CHAPTER FOUR

When it came to romancing a woman, Lucas preferred nice and slow, mostly because he usually liked to get to know the person first. His job was all about precision, planning and practice. War might be nasty business but a SEAL team incision was all about stealthy attacks.

He'd applied this philosophy in his pursuit of female company—methodical and somewhat predictable because he was, after all, a SEAL. It'd never cross his mind that he wouldn't succeed.

That wasn't happening with Kit.

From the moment he'd set eyes on her, there was this urgency to go after her. Male instinct told him to claim and to claim quickly. He didn't question why. From the get-go, he just knew this wasn't going to be nice and slow.

He prided himself as a pretty uncomplicated male. Don't just talk. Do. Don't just explain. Show. Don't beat around the bush. Make it clear, mow it down.

Yeah, he didn't have much use for words.

He could sum up his current thoughts in a couple of caveman sentences. Want Kit. Take Kit. Claim Kit.

A nice hotel room would just have to do instead of a cave.

Actually, this woman was leading the charge. She took the keys from the desk clerk. She led him to the room. She turned the key and tugged at his hand to come in after her. Okay, he kicked the door shut. But that was it. He quite enjoyed letting a woman order him around. Their jackets were already on the floor.

"Take off your shirt," she said.

He obediently did so, pulling it over his head. Her smile made him want to rip her sweater off her but he stayed still as she ran bold hands through his chest hair.

"Lower, please," Lucas requested.

"I like your chest hair. I like to play with it."

"They don't give me the same pleasure as other parts of me," he explained. He placed his hand over hers and slid it down over the steely bulge in his pants. His cock expanded some more, eager for more pleasure. "See? This part of me has hair too. And there is something there for you to play with."

Her eyes twinkled with amusement. "And what could that be?"

"Something big. Hard. And I heard, quite enjoyable."

"Take off your pants, then."

"Thought you'd never ask," he said, and did what came from years of training—unzip, tug, kick pants away. All SEAL, all commando. And his team's motto: standing and ready for action.

She looked down for a long moment, then her gaze came back up to meet his. Her eyes were very wide. She licked her moist lips.

"Is that why they call you Cucumber?"

Lucas smiled slowly. SEALs' nicknames were given to them by their own platoon, usually after a physical attribute or an embarrassing moment. His came from a combo of both.

"Kinda. Do you really want me to tell you a bedtime story now? I'd rather have you undress so I can tuck you into bed."

She lifted her arms. "Go for it, sailor."

He didn't need to be asked twice. Her top came off in one swift pull and he threw it over his shoulder. She had on some frilly black bra. She unbuttoned her pants and they fell to the floor, then she turned and ran towards the bed.

He watched her luscious ass for a long moment. Praise the Lord for inventing thongs. And after his brain cells settled back down, he leapt after her.

She bounced onto the bed. He dropped on his knees behind her, and tucking an arm around her waist, he stopped her from turning over. That sexy ass was too beautiful a sight.

"Don't move just yet," he said, fitting his hands on the round cheeks.

So smooth. He bent down and took a nibble. His hand, tucked under her, slipped inside the flimsy thong. She gasped as he cupped her.

He slowly slid the elastic aside, intimately brushing against her, priming her. He was a big guy. It was important to get a woman really ready for him. She was wet already. He teased her some more while he took his time nibbling the back of her thighs and the gorgeous silky-smooth ass until he had her squirming.

"Cupcake, I'm going to taste you first," he murmured, slowly turning her around.

He pulled the thong aside with one finger. Beautiful. The kind of rosy pink he liked. Her wetness beckoned, whetting his appetite, and he slid another finger down slowly, exploring her slickness. She made a strangled sound and fell back on the bed. Yeah, like that. Just the way he wanted, with all the juicy parts within easy reach. He put both hands on her thighs and spread her legs a little more, then leaned in, placing his mouth on the exposed pink flesh.

He heard some muffled sounds from her as her lower body jerked up. His firm hold on her thighs kept her from escaping his lips. So lusciously wet. So deliciously sweet. Her soft moans and thrusts to his face sent electric jolts right down to his rock-hard cock, impatiently waiting its turn. A woman was meant to moan like that for a man.

He tongued her slit and pushed upward, looking for that nub. Yeah, there it was, the little pearl waiting for his attention. He kissed it and rolled his tongue around, adjusting the pressure on her clit as he checked her reaction.

"Lucas!" She squirmed at one point.

Jackpot. He wanted her squirming and moaning his name.

"What?" He whispered, in between licks.

"Lu...cas! I'm...going to come."

He laughed quietly. "Ladies first, baby."

He went in for the kill, sliding one finger inside her as he continued stroking her with his tongue, this time not bothering to answer her when she choked out his name again.

Her rapid breathing became little throaty cries. He gently sucked the hood hiding that little pearl between her legs. Her hands gripped his hair as she came hard. Then she went limp. Her damp release excited him unbearably and he gave her one last flick with his tongue before getting off his knees slowly and going to get his pants.

She lay there panting, looking at him as he sheathed on a condom over his very hard, about to burst, erection. He strode back to her.

"My turn, babe," he said.

* * *

Kit languorously stretched, and using her legs, slid higher on the bed, opening her arms to invite the tall, impressive-looking man to come to her. Oh God, but he was a big, muscular hunk. Everything in her world had turned into small, unimportant stuff since they'd met.

All the advice her brothers had given her.

All her careful planning about taking her time with relationships after the last fiasco.

All the usual "don't give the guy what he wants or he won't come back" girlie chitchat.

Whoosh. Out the window. She wanted Lucas Branson in a way she'd never felt before. It started as a hot flush of awareness, that initial attraction, which then bloomed into a cloud of heat and desire that seemed to weigh down on all the calm, oh-so-sensible advice in her brain. All Lucas had to do was put his arms around her, enveloping her with his irresistible male scent, and that cloud had exploded and she'd let all her wants and needs rain down on her.

Free. Uncaring. Total abandonment.

She wanted this man and she would have him.

His erection stood proud and straight as he put on protection. Something squeezed tightly in her loins. She wanted a taste of that later, but right now....

She unsnapped her bra, freeing her breasts from the cups. His dark eyes looked on, mesmerized by her movements. Then she wiggled her index finger, beckoning him.

He climbed over her, his nakedness emanating heat, his cock looking even bigger this close. He groaned when she reached down and circled her hands around his erection.

"Don't squeeze too hard, Cupcake," he said, as he leaned forward, caging each side of her with his big, muscular arms. "You don't want me to come before I'm inside you."

She lifted her legs, angling her body beneath him. "Hurry, hurry, hurry," she breathed.

His thrust was slow and steady. She wriggled, gasping as the pressure of his entry expanded her vagina. He slid out and thrust again, this time going in deeper. He repeated. Deeper. Oh, God, deeper even. Her neck snapped back when he gave another thrust, his thighs hitting her ass as he pushed in all the way.

"You okay?" His voice came out in a growl.

She chuckled. "Is that all you got, big boy?"

He just shook his head and leaned forward more, shifting his weight to his elbows, rolling her lower body higher until she had to wrap her legs around his waist. He pushed so deep inside her, she felt faint from the intense pressure.

"More?" He whispered.

She was never one to back away from a challenge. "I thought SEALs could go in much, much deeper," she whispered back, "when they plan to detonate something."

He looked down at her, his eyes gleaming in the half-light. "Saucy woman. So many ways to detonate, so little time. Cupcake, prepare to explode," he told her as he started to move.

Kit hung on to the broad shoulders, feeling the tensing of muscles as he demonstrated how deep he could go and for how long. She'd never thought herself very sensitive down there but now she felt *everything*. Each stroke massaged sensitive nerves she never knew existed, making her clench her internal muscles in delight. The sensation of being taken excited her tremendously and his little bites of her neck, right under the ear, weakened her so, building the heat between her legs.

Every time he pushed inside her, his thick length rubbed against her clitoris and some other secret part inside. Her whole body sang with pleasure at each slide and the tension from the need to release grew like a hot-air balloon being filled. Any moment now, she would take flight. She could hear herself crying out his name again until her words were just incomprehensible syllables.

The bed creaked under them as he continued the sure and steady pace. She wanted him to hurry but he seemed intent on just prolonging the building ecstasy. Her eyes closed as the tension built and built from the pull and push of his thrusts

Now.

Now!

Her whole body tightened and arched up. Then her whole being let go and it felt like a free fall through space. His pace became faster as he matched her frantic urging. She heard his deep groans and his body, slippery with perspiration, enveloped her as he climaxed with her.

Seconds went by. She couldn't move at all. Not that she could, with him sprawled on top of her, his face buried in her neck. What a lovely, lovely feeling, to come together like that.

She had been wrong all this time, thinking sex was just Tab A fitting Tab B, with some fleeting feeling from the connection. Absolutely, wonderfully wrong.

Kit smiled contentedly. There was so much feeling. So much heat. All along, she just needed someone she really desired, someone with a marvelously big cock. The thought of him leaving made her sigh. She wished she could keep him to herself.

His hand was between her legs again, lazily stroking her. She jerked up because she was still sensitive.

"Shhhh." He crooned in her ear. "Don't fight it. I can take you higher, baby. This time, you're going to scream for me."

It was an unbearable teasing as he made sure she stayed relaxed. Every time she tensed up, his stroking slowed down to a gentle glide. Everything became focused on where he was touching, how slowly he stoked her fire, each slide of his finger like an expert cellist making his instrument sing. And did she ever. She couldn't stop the throaty cries escaping her lips as her lower body burned with desire. Every upward sensation brought a mounting ecstasy and every descent made her shiver with anticipation. And when he finally pushed two fingers inside her, she screamed, her orgasm finally bursting into full flames. His mouth covered hers as his fingers continued their magic.

Much, much later, wrapped in Lucas arms, she heard her cell phone's familiar text whistle. She tried to get up and the arms tightened.

"Where are you going?" His sleepy, satiated voice tickled her ear.

"Read my text message. It's probably Kit and the boys, wondering where we are."

He heaved a sigh, then turned over. "Guess I better check mine too, then. What do you want to do? Get back with them or stay in bed and party on our own? I opt for more Cupcake."

Hmm. She wanted more Cucumber. "You'll be too tired to get back to work tomorrow," she teased.

"I've been up all night before, babe."

His husky laugh made her shiver with its sexy promise.

She got off the bed and headed for their pile of clothes. She searched his pocket and then came back to bed, handing him his phone.

"I'll tell my guys DND," Lucas told her.

"DND?"

"Do not disturb."

"They'll know what we're doing for sure, then," she said, as she looked at her phone. "Yup, it's Lulu, telling me the movie is over and..."

She laughed, shook her head and texted back.

"What?"

"Oh, nothing."

She put the phone on the night table and flung herself on top of that hot body. "Everything's fine. Let's see how long you can stay up all night."

She reached for him. He was hard already. She slid lower, giving him an idea what was coming.

"My guys won't tell Lulu what DND is. What did you text to her?"

"You sound a bit...strained. Are you sure you can stay up all night? Maybe you want to rest up?"

There was a short silence as she took the head of his cock in her mouth and rolled her tongue across it several times.

"Test me," he finally said. "Continue what you're doing."

She grinned. She thought she could distract him from asking too much about his sister. Lulu was busy. Her text had made her laugh because it read, "DND, Kit. Distract my brother for me!"

DND. She wondered whether Lulu got that term from being around SEALs too long. She had a fair idea with whom she was busy right now.

She slowly took the full erection deep in her mouth, carefully coming down as far as she could. He was so big, she doubted if she could take it all in, but she did her best, grasping the thick shaft and swallowing deeply. A very male groan followed that. If she could have smiled, she would. Because she wanted to give the man as much pleasure as he'd given her earlier, she tried something she'd never done before. Massaging his balls, she gave a very light tug and at the same time, relaxing her throat, she took him deeply into her mouth. She was immediately rewarded.

"Fuck. Baby. I...Hot...God...Baby!"

She let go, inhaled, then repeated what she just did.

"Uh. Gooooood, man-fuck-take-umm-unngh-more-FFFUCK!"

Kit wanted to laugh. Reducing the always-in-control Lucas Branson into incoherent mumbling was fun. Oh, she didn't mind the task of distracting him at all.

PART TWO

CHAPTER FIVE

Four weeks later.
Pakistan-Afghan mountainous border

Seven seconds. That was how long a SEAL usually had to distinguish between the bad guys and the good ones in a small space and do the appropriate damage.

Lucas had done numerous recon raids, but he noted this was the first time he'd assaulted an enemy first by the smell of chicken and god-knows-what shit. He, Dirk and Mink had crawled into the target's courtyard through a hole in the animals' barn and had found themselves underneath some kind of long chicken cage. The space was so low, they had to remove their helmets to stop from clacking the bottom of the coop. They startled a few birds as they did a long belly crawl among sleeping chickens, picking up all the slimy bird poop on their clothes, face, hair...everywhere. And startled birds pooped some more. Warm stinking stuff slid down his unprotected neck as he maneuvered his big body through the tight space, not uttering a sound as something that smelled really bad splattered on his nose.

He supposed it could have been worse. Could have had to swim through a pig's trough. They made their way silently towards the front. It wasn't very dark; the light from outside shone through the cracks in the building.

The darkness in the barn was punctured as they kicked down the door leading to the courtyard where their targets were having some kind of barbeque party. The first gasps at their appearance weren't exactly blood-curdling screams of pain or panic. Nope. The four people near the entrance to the barn gagged at the smell of excrement emanating from the three intruders.

Yeah, a SEAL had all kinds of deadly weapons at his disposal at any given moment. He liked the idea of killing a few enemies by just smelling them to death.

Seven seconds. In that flash, his brain quickly registered the screaming women and a couple of kids running back towards the main house, away from the area around the barn. He knew, from hours and hours of prep as well as close quarters target identification training, in the mountains, the womenfolk usually sat away from the men. So he quickly adjusted, pointing his weapon the other direction.

Their insider had been right after all. The team had scratched their heads over his instructions to attack near the animals. Wouldn't the wedding be inside? But like Dirk had suggested, maybe it was a barbecue party. This made their attack easier. Their Intel had also noted that the other male family members who lived there would be attending the ceremony, thus all the other quarters nearby would be empty. The gathering was the perfect time to surround the hostiles in one spot, giving the SEALs the advantage of taking them down and bringing in their target.

"Team Bravo reporting, infiltration completed. Males to your right," he spoke into his mic, informing his commander the needed information for direct insertion. "Team Charlie, males at seven o'clock but females are at five o'clock."

"Team Alpha, go!" Hawk, his leader, gave the command over the mic. "Team Charlie, go!"

Lucas, Dirk and Mink's first role was to distract the outside guards and enough inside targets so the other two teams could climb up the wall surrounding the courtyard. Hawk, Zone and Turner were Team Alpha; Jazz and Joker were Team Charlie.

Lucas popped off the first two men who had picked up their-nearby weapons. He knew Mink and Dirk were taking care of his six so he walked forward, looking for the target, Yakob, whom they'd given the codename "The Cob" for communications.

Their insider Intel had been very clear. Their target would be in ceremonial clothing, bright with lots of gold. He should be easy to find.

"The Cob sighted, over," Lucas reported.

Team Alpha was already on top of the wall ahead. Lucas could see Hawk rappelling down while Zone was taking out the few guards nearby.

"I see him, over," Hawk said in his ear piece.

"I'll cover you."

The rat-tat-tat of gun fire multiplied exponentially in the next seconds. In an extraction raid, the element of surprise was the most important advantage. Go in, hit your targets, let the chosen teammate do his job as extractor, get out. There should be no pauses at all to allow the other side to regroup.

Out of the corner of his eye, Lucas caught sight of something bright where Team Alpha was situated. It should be dark over there. He swung his weapon around, ready to come to his teammate's defense.

And paused.

It was a—

"Don't shoot. Female climbing our rope." It was Zone, still positioned on the wall.

A bullet zinged past, causing Lucas to jerk away reactively, and a knife embedded itself on the weapon strap around his waist. It stung.

Like hell if he was going get himself shot dead with bird crap all over him.

No time to think. Back to the business at hand. Zone could handle one lone female.

Lucas charged forward, using the ceremonial tables and brightly wrapped poles as protection, as he took out the enemy with surgical efficiency. He rolled under a table to get to the other side, closer to the main participants of the ceremonial party. His instructions had been clear—if Team Alpha failed in its attempt to nab The Cob from behind the group, his team had the responsibility to get to the target from the front side. A more difficult goal at the moment because of the obstacles strewn between them and the target.

"Team Charlie reporting. Exit secured and open, over," Jazz's voice announced over the mic.

"Team Alpha reporting. We got the Cob. Cover us, over," Hawk said. "Cumber?"

"Ready!" Lucas confirmed.

Lucas pulled down the special gas mask that had been secured under his thin hood to protect it from being pulled off by the wires sticking out from under the chicken cages. Thank the Lord for some quick thinking there or they'd have been smeared with bird crap too.

A flashbang was discharged. It exploded in the central courtyard, the noise and sudden light creating panic among the partygoers. Lucas rolled two small CS canisters into the targeted area.

There was a quick barrage of gunfire and then an odd silence as all the male hostiles were momentarily incapacitated. Everyone in the vicinity without a gas mask was down. And then the coughing and choking began.

They had used a minimal dose of CS gas, just enough to create panic and confusion so they could make a quick escape. There were too many women and children around to take down all the men, even though the women of this culture were traditionally separated. Also, not all the men belonged to the terrorist cell the SEALs were after, only those around the Cob.

"Alpha, Team Bravo got your back, over," Lucas said. "Mink, flank left. Dirk, to the right. Confirm positions, over."

"Affirmative," their voices said in unison.

The familiar figures of Hawk and Turner jogged past them, each dragging a prisoner. Lucas' team followed, guarding the rear.

Jazz and Turner beckoned from the open exit and they disappeared through it with the prisoners. Lucas and Dirk fired shots to keep any attackers from behind at bay. Mink threw a fire pellet into a bale of hay near the entrance, setting it on fire—distraction for those who might run after them. Zone appeared out of nowhere, having left his position on top of the wall at some point. He was alone. No time to question him about that strange female who climbed the rope.

The team had mapped out the escape route from the compound after the first recon to check out the terrain. The path, well worn by horses and carts, veered off precariously and wasn't suitable for a quick run with two reluctant bodies. They had instead chosen the river as transport and had made the necessary arrangements.

Lucas followed his SEAL squad, constantly turning around to eye the rear. The dark was their friend as the enemy would need lights to search for them. Easy to detect. They were making more noise than usual, though, what with dragging along two reluctant men. Neither was calling for help. Hmm. Hawk must have taken the time to gag them.

Lucas grinned in the dark. He would have to ask his commander whether he had given the bride a kiss since he appeared to have plenty of time to gag the asshole.

Jazz whistled softly and not far away, a whistle replied back. An engine rumbled to life. The shadow of the Special Operations Craft-Riverine boat they had ordered appeared out of the darkness, illuminated by only one pinpoint of light.

Lucas' team hurriedly boarded. It wouldn't be long before any nearby Yakob men and allies who might be rushing toward the courtyard heard the SOC-R and start signaling their river guards. Recon extraction over. The fun had begun.

Hawk and a few others shoved the two prisoners into the boat and the shadow crew on board pulled them up. They were members of Special Boat Team 22, all elite Special Warfare Combatant-craft Crewmen. Lucas and his team had worked with them before and relied on their water-navigating skills many a time while on hydrographic recons.

One of them patted Lucas on the back—three taps— signaling his identity. Lucas returned the greeting with a familiar nudge of his elbow as he positioned himself and his weapon. No words needed. River Devil was one of his close friends from the Naval Academy. Good to have him by his side in combat.

They zoomed off into the murky darkness. The noise they were making would only give them enough time to get far out enough—glints of lights to the left, moving shadows and yeah, Lucas fancied he could hear a lot of shouting going on—before the situation became noisy.

"Showtime," Mink shouted into his ear.

Lucas crouched low.

The SOC-R was equipped with five guns that could go 360 degrees. Good luck, terrorist dudes. In the face of enemy attack, the SWCC response, in military speak, was usually "violence of action." No finesse at all, Lucas mused, but hey, it got the job done, so no complaints from him.

"Contact!" A voice he recognized as Devil's shouted. That was standard command for 'Yoohoo, bastards, here we come!'

A deafening torrent of gunfire pounded all around them. Water rose up like a moving magic curtain from the spray of bullets. There was some return fire but Lucas doubted that would last too long.

In front, Zone and Turner pushed the two prisoners down as shell casings from the tremendous show of firepower started to fall all around them. The fog of smoke from the weapons burned the back of Lucas' throat. He helped to feed the ammo, his gaze following the plumes of smoke on the bank, signifying the demolished targets. The river wasn't very wide so the best defense was to keep shooting. One never knew whether there were hostiles crawling along the banks. With the help of night-vision goggles and high-tech equipment, the lookout man gave directions and warnings of sighted targets.

Lucas shoved away a pile of spent slugs and bullet casings that had landed at his feet, making room. The boat began to speed up, taking off down river. The thumping of gunfire became less and less sporadic. Wedding party over, folks.

The rest of the trip went without incident. Everyone was still on high alert, with no small talk other than greeting and acknowledgement. Lucas could hear his commander, Hawk, speaking quietly with the boat crew commander, then watched curiously as they walked back and pulled the Cob—he recognized him by his shiny clothing—into a sitting position before placing a hood over his head. As soon as he was secured that way, the other prisoner sat up without help and Hawk leaned over and cut his ropes. The man rubbed his wrists, shaking away the stiffness, but neither man exchanged any words.

What the hell?

"Separate the prisoners when we arrive and ship them to the assigned detainment cells," Hawk said. "No communicating with anyone where each prisoner is to be held."

"Yes, sir!"

Lucas watched the freed prisoner hand his commander a note. Clearly, the order just given was bullshit being fed to the Cob or he'd eat his shoe. Lucas made a face. Okay, not his currently shit-infested shoe, but one that was sitting on a shelf back home. Home made him think of Kit-Ling. He immediately shut that door mentally. Think of that wild woman and he'd get his pants tight from a hard-on. He had done that so many times since Charleston, he was beginning to wonder what was wrong with him. One couldn't afford to lose focus out here in the field or chance being killed.

The rest of the trip back to base was uneventful. The well-guarded US-controlled canal was a welcome sight and Lucas found his tenseness dissipating. He cricked his neck and relaxed his grip on his weapon. If he were lucky, he could actually get a shower tonight. He sniffed himself. Right now he'd settle for a quick dip in the canal.

They gathered as a group, both his team and the special ops boat crew. An interpreter met with Hawk and after an exchange of instructions, the Cob was marched off, with guards holding him on both sides. Interestingly enough, the other prisoner just stood there with his guards. He was definitely local but much taller, more Lucas' size, actually. And he seemed very comfortable standing there, quietly taking in the scene with an impassive face. Lucas doubted any of his team mates were deceived by the easy stance. This man knew how to fight.

Someone called out his name. He turned and high-fived his buds. Mink and Dirk did a chest bump. His friend, River Devil, looking appropriately devilish with his face streaked in green and black and tufts of his red hair falling out of his head gear, gave him a fist bump.

"I'd hug you, man, but not with that fucking garbage truck stench," he said, grinning. "What did you do, frogman, swim in their sewage?"

The others laughed as they studied the three men from Team Bravo.

"Stooges, you look and smell like shit," Jazz remarked, sniffing the air. The tall and lean Cajun grinned wickedly. "Can't wait to hear your report."

"You have a knife sticking out of you, Cumber," Hawk pointed out conversationally. "Must not be hurting too much."

Lucas looked down. Sure enough, that darn blade was still embedded in his belt and yeah, part of it was still inside him.

"Not hurting at all, sir," he told his commander. "Blade's barely in."

"His big balls deflected most of it," Mink explained and they all laughed again.

Hawk turned to the "prisoner" who still stood there in silence. "He's out of hearing. Thank you for all your Intel. Did you get what you wanted?"

Ah. He was their inside guy.

The man nodded. "I got the name of the buyer from Yakob. I'll need to use a satellite feed to pass it on to Number Nine."

Lucas' ears pricked up. Number Nine. Wasn't that the COS Commando they'd met in Asia, the one with the strange eyes? So this dude was part of that outfit. These COS commandos and his team had crossed each other's paths a lot lately. Not surprising, since they were fighting the same people, only with different goals.

"You can use my private one," Hawk offered.

"Thank you."

"Everyone meet up in thirty minutes at Debriefing. Cumber, if you need to sew that up first, let me know, but definitely wipe off some of that shit before entering the war room." Hawk's serious expression broke into a smile. "All three from Team Bravo. Miss Hutchens would appreciate it."

Amber Hutchens was Hawk's fiancé and also an Intel asset, supplying information on illegal weapons dealings and their international routes. Not too long ago, she'd played a major role in helping the SEALs locate some caches of weapons hidden in Croatia. That's where she and Hawk had met and Lucas had known, from the look in his commander's eyes whenever Amber Hutchens was around, that his bachelor days were numbered.

"Aye, sir!"

"I'll see you all in thirty, then. Follow me, Shahrukh, Jazz."

The insider, Jazz and Hawk walked off.

"Someone's wedding party sure ended with a bang," River Devil remarked. "You guys made quite a noise. We were thinking the Cob's men might be closer to the river to get you guys when you ran so we set some traps, just in case, bro."

"Aw, you river cowboys were worried about us. You do care!" Mink joked.

"Nah. We didn't feel like working too hard tonight rescuing your frog asses," someone quipped back.

"It's good to have everything work out as planned," Lucas agreed, "except for the damn chicken cages."

"Phoowee. Get the fuck out of here and take care of that wound too, will you? Fucking gagging me to death, you three," Turner said.

Zone shook his head, poking Mink with a stick and holding up some smelly piece of crap that had been dangling over his shoulder. "Trust the stooges to get themselves in shit."

Lucas shrugged. He didn't mind being made fun of— they got the job done. That was all that mattered.

"See you in a few. Peace out." He, Mink and Dirk were heading to the clean-up area when he remembered. "Hey, I forgot to ask Zone about that girl climbing up the wall. What was that all about?"

Dirk shrugged. "Beats me. I saw Zone helping her up."

"She didn't come with us, though," Mink said. "Nice strong legs."

"You had time to look at her legs?" Lucas asked.

Mink grinned. "Hey, I looked over there and there they were."

"You'd better not boast about that too loudly, bro. The native men will kill you for insulting their females"

"Yeah, watch your mouth," Lucas said.

"I know, Cumber, I know. We'll talk about other things, yes?"

They bantered on as they undid all the weaponry and gear strapped to their bodies. Lucas yanked the knife out of the strap around his waist, studying the short blade for a moment before throwing it in the pile. They stripped off soiled clothes in record time, kicking them under the shower, letting the water wash away as much of the animal crap as possible.

"Shit, man, you need stitches for that," Dirk said, pointing down.

Lucas checked. The knife had gone through the strap sideways, embedded in the skin near his waist between his belly button and hip, deep enough to cause a little damage.

"Meh. Just give me a Band-Aid."

"Dude, you're bleeding. Take care of it."

"Don't want to miss the meeting. I'll let you sew me up later." Mink was the medic on their team. "Then you can tell my sis you saved my life and she'll kiss you again."

Mink gave him a wink. "You're a generous brother. I'll tell Kit you nearly died and she'll kiss you better too."

"Damn, I feel all lonesome without someone to kiss me," Dirk said, throwing a bar of soap at Mink. "Here, wash my back and make me feel better."

* * *

"How are you doing?"

Kit looked up from writing an email on her tablet in a moving vehicle. They would soon be out in the countryside and wireless connection would be spotty. She wanted to reply to Lucas' email—if you could call a three-word sentence mail—before she took a nap. Normally, she would look out of the window and take in the view but it was pitch black outside and the others had advised her to sleep because tomorrow would be a busy day.

Sean Cortez sat across from her, long legs stretched out. The light from his tablet illuminated his face, making his watchful dark eyes gleam. Kit wished she had half his energy—the man was seemingly indefatigable, always up and about interviewing people, making plans for clandestine meetings and taping reports for the news service for which they worked. She was determined to copy his non-stop pace, even though almost everyone on the team had assured her she wasn't the only one having a tough time keeping up with Sean and that he didn't expect them to follow his schedule.

Other than talking to the man on the other side of the camera when she was in the States, she'd never met the celebrated road journalist in person before. Face-to-face, he was just as she'd imagined—bigger than life, intense about his work, and a demanding teammate. She'd applied to be on his team this time as part of her expanded work load precisely because of his focus and passion about his projects. Working on his team would teach her a lot more about international field work as a journalist.

So far, he'd kept her busy reading up on the Afghan-Pakistan border and its history and people. When they had a few spare moments, he'd quizzed her knowledge, always pointing out her wrong assumptions about people and culture. So much so that now, every time he asked her anything, she would give his question detailed consideration before replying.

"As in how am I at this moment?" she asked. "Or, how am I doing at my new job? Or, how am I doing in a general life sort of way?"

He laughed quietly. "You have a different answer for all three conditions?"

"Of course. Unless you just want the standard 'I'm fine, thank you' reply but then why ask in the middle of nowhere, right?"

"Right. So, should I reply for you myself or are you going to answer me?"

Kit looked down at her tablet. Some men were so prickly. No sense of humor at all. Not like Lucas Branson, who made her laugh so much for three days.

I miss Cupcake.

That line made her want to giggle again. What a ridiculous nickname. Besides, that was the name *she* used on him; somehow, it'd ended up being hers. Of course, how did one top Cucumber as a nickname? Well, she too could be short and sweet.

She typed: "*I miss Cucumber*" and hit send, then looked up at the man still studying and patiently waiting for her to say something.

"At this moment," she said, "I'm just chilling. As for my new job, I think I'm doing quite well, getting the hang of working in a culture where women are second-class citizens. As for my general well-being, I don't think it's of any interest to you. Satisfied?"

"Of course your general well-being is of interest to me," Sean said. He looked down, frowned and tapped on his tablet. His attention still on his screen, he murmured, "If it weren't, I wouldn't ask. You seemed so at ease with your new responsibilities. I'm very impressed with your prep work and the way you handled talking with the locals."

Surprised, she stopped checking her Inbox. From just a few weeks with him 24/7, she knew praise coming from Sean Cortez was a rare thing. "Thanks," she said.

"You told me when we started you wanted to learn about international field work. Are you ready to dip your foot in the water?"

"I thought that's what I've been doing." Part of her job had been scouting where the women folk gathered and seeing who indicated an interest in talking to the journalists.

"We'll be out of the Swat Valley district tomorrow. There won't be much contact with the locals because they're more traditional in the mountains, especially with foreigners. Do you know why I picked you as part of the team? Besides your excellent resume and ability to communicate as a public info officer, of course."

Her tablet was buzzing. That was quick. Lucas was sending a private message.

"I'm not as dumb as you think. You picked me because of my looks." Kit grinned. "That came out wrong."

Sean smiled back, amusement stamped on his face. "I think you like to tease, Kit." He shifted in his seat. "But you're right. You blend in with the locals, especially when you wear their clothes, and I wanted to take advantage of...your looks."

"Ha. Knew it." No doubt about it, because of her mixed Asian facial features, she had been able to get the

Pashtun women to feel comfortable enough to talk to her through a female interpreter. She glanced down at her tablet again.

I can't talk tonite. Debriefing. Not that kind.

She quickly typed back. *Aw. I'm not dirty-minded like you. I can't talk either. No Internet soon. On field work. Will you text me soon?*

Doing anything interesting?

They couldn't talk much about their work, especially him, so everything was always vague.

I'm flirting with my team top guy. What about you? Anything interesting to report?

Someone soaped my back.

Oooh. You win. I hope to do that to your back one day soon.

Keep that thought, Cupcake. Got to go.

TTYL.

Kit signed off, feeling satisfied she got to talk to Lucas. Wherever he was, he had been busy, doing what SEALs do. It'd been almost a week since they last had a chat. She missed their quick back and forth texts. They had even Skyped a couple of times so they could have longer conversations, which tended to become hot and heavy after a while. Their mutual attraction hadn't dissipated at all. A smile from him, even from a laptop image, would brighten her day. It was scary and exciting to feel this way about someone again.

"That's not a smile about work, I bet," Sean said dryly.

Kit looked up, startled. She'd totally forgotten about him.

"Sorry. I was multi-tasking, doing last minute stuff since I'm sure we won't be able to find a wireless hotspot out in the countryside."

Sean pointed to his tablet. "Same here. Were you talking to your boyfriend?"

Kit frowned. Boyfriend? Lucas and she were...what were they? Somewhere between friends and lovers. Or maybe more. She would like them to be more.

"Just a friend," she replied instead. "And also emailing my mom. She's a bit protective and if I don't tell her I'd be incommunicado for a few days, she'd be sending a search party."

Sean chuckled. "It'd be tough to look for you in these mountains. Swat Valley is a beautiful touristy place but the mountains, it's a different story. Your mom would need a different kind of search party out there."

Yeah, like my brother. He's a—and she grinned because Lucas' voice came to her mind loud and clear—*fucking Airborne Ranger.* Oh, she was in so much trouble. That man was haunting her thoughts.

"You haven't met my Mom. She's very tiny but she always gets things done her way. The men in my family fear her wrath." She laughed. Her mother was so typically cliché Chinese dragon lady, she suspected it was mostly an act. "She's very good at wheedling information out of my brothers and me."

"So you got that from her."

Kit looked at Sean again in surprise. "Hey, full of compliments tonight. I'll take it, Mr. Cortez." She cocked her head. "Now, tell me what information you're wanting me to try to get."

Sean leaned forward and beckoned her to do the same so he could lower his voice even more. Curious, she did so.

"The teenager we're going to meet with tomorrow—Minah—I need you to ask her about her groom, or rather, groom-to-be."

"The interview would cover that, right?" Kit asked. Because of an opportunity presented by one of Sean's sources, they'd decided to include *swara*, the custom of giving away a girl as payment for an offense, in their investigative report on the recent killing of a famous Pashtun singer by traditionalists. "We have the names. What else?"

"The name interests me. I need you to delve deeper into the crime committed by her family against the groom."

"Okay."

"Go beyond what she's going to tell you. I want more information about the groom, his clan, his whereabouts."

"How would we connect our feature on the murdered singer with his background?" The Pashtun woman, popular among the city and country folks, and her father were gunned down. "I know her death was an assassination ordered by her former husband, who, from my interviews with the women, made me understand he'd felt humiliated and needed to restore his honor."

That was why they were going to meet with this young girl, who, reportedly, had just been given away to an older man to restore family honor. They were going to weave the themes together as part of the investigation. The plan was to tie both stories to show how marriages were arranged and their consequences to the women involved.

"Latifah's death might have been officially attributed to her husband. Although there's no proof, I have reasons to believe the murder had Taliban-connected elements and I want to look at it from another angle."

Whoa. "That would change the focus of our investigation."

Sean shrugged. "I've changed my mind before. My sources told me this young girl's husband, or whatever you want to call him, has radical connections. Some kind of middleman for the warlords and that he has many other side-dealings that had to do with all the skirmishes in the war zone."

"But what about the women's plight?" That was Kit's main reason she had wanted to be on this team, for this particular project. The subject matter was different from the usual political topics. "What about Latifah's story? And all the other women's stories that I've gathered?"

Sean eyed her quizzically for a second and leaned over so close, his breath was hot against her ear. "You can have total control of that part of the report, if you get me the information I want from our girl tomorrow."

Then he straightened back up and sat back against his seat, eyeing her contemplatively. Kit stared back at him, not at all sure what this all meant.

"Sleep on it," he continued. He turned his attention back to his tablet and tapped a few times. "We have time."

From then on, he appeared to be immersed in his work and Kit didn't feel like asking more questions in loud whispers. The two interpreters were sleeping in the far end of the van, where they had arranged their sleeping bags over the longer seats. The cameraman and photographer were sitting in front with their guide. She could hear the murmurs, indicating they were still awake. Their own quiet conversation was a normal thing for the others because they had to conduct many of their meetings this way. Once they were out of the more touristy areas, being seen together in public too much would only invite trouble since none of them were married to each other, nor did they have any chaperones. All they had were international guides who arranged their meetings and were expected to sit in as "chaperones." So when necessary, they had mostly used their laptops and cameras as a way to hold their more private get-togethers about details they had gathered, but that still hadn't felt secure enough.

In the morning, they would be exchanging vehicles, going in two, rather than one, so as not to offend the Pashtun elders who were at the camps set up by the Red Cross and international peace organizations for displaced Pashtuns. These people were without homes due to the many bloody skirmishes in the region. Kit and her team's plan was for the men to stay in the male side of the camp and take photographs while she and the female interpreter met with the women bringing the young girl. They were told there was a small building where they could set up a formal interview too.

Kit got up, pulling out a small pillow from her rucksack. She made herself as comfortable as she could. Letting her mind wander as she relaxed into sleep, it went to her favorite topic of fantasy these days—Lucas Branson. She wondered where he was—must be somewhere civilized, since he mentioned soap. Of course, he could have been lying. Sleepily, she hoped he was just kidding about someone soaping his back, since that would mean a woman was around to do that. She didn't think he would let Mink or Dirk soap his back. She grinned in the dark at that image. Now, that would be a great blackmail photo for Lulu.

In spite of the challenges of being in a long distance relationship, she and Lucas had grown to know quite a bit about each other. They'd planned on meeting again as soon as he was able to take a few days off and this time, they were going to spend some private time without their gang of friends. She looked forward to that a lot. It was crazy, but she missed touching him.

She'd learned quite a bit more about him through their communication too. He always asked her what she was doing at that moment. When she'd asked why, the answer was, as usual, simple and direct.

Want to see you in my head, especially doing something normal.

Why? She'd asked again.

It relaxes me after a day of shooting at someone.

Kit yawned, letting go of consciousness with a final thought. Whatever would he think if he knew she was in Afghanistan among government insurgents and mountain warlords? He wouldn't be so relaxed then, she would bet.

CHAPTER SIX

Lucas looked around. The war room was crowded, with two teams coming in—four or five actually, if one counted the contract agents—and seemed more so once the large screen filled up with the bigger-than-life video feed of Admiral Madison. There were only two women in the room—termed contract operatives over here, since some of the men weren't familiar with them. Amber Hutchens and Vivi Verreau-Zeringue, members of the Joint Task Force which Admiral Madison had formed some time ago to get better Intel for his SEALs, were there. Ever since compromised Intel from the CIA had caused a SEAL squad to be killed in action, the admiral had taken to working with even more underground networks.

The move had paid off, netting Dragan Dilaver, the one responsible for the SEAL deaths, among other international crimes, with the help of Amber Hutchens. She was what Lucas would term, one hot chica. And she was also Hawk's fiancée. His team commander had met her during the Dilaver operation and had fallen in love.

Not only beautiful, but one hell of a fighter too. Lucas recalled when the team had learned how she'd saved Hawk's life all by herself, with a big bag of weapons and some grenades. Right now, she was bent over helping the tech get the live feed to work properly, giving the roomful of appreciative male eyes a nice view of...Lucas looked away, pulling a chair out, and nodding at Mink and Dirk to join in. They were gazing raptly at Miss Hutchens too and he gave them a meaningful look. They shrugged and came over. Okay, so it wasn't politically correct to check out any women in the war room, especially one his own commander was about to marry, but thank the Lord for hot and capable women, anyway.

Mink echoed his thoughts. He leaned over and whispered, "Pity we can't make remarks about both women. Taken."

Dirk nodded. "Taken *down*," he said, in a mournful voice. "All casualties on our side too, dammit. Miss Hutchens has Hawk's number. Jazz went down easy. And there's Joker pining for his hot mama. Zone's revealed he's going out with a senator's daughter. Cumber's got Kit on his mind. We're being taken down one by one."

"Kit and I just met," Lucas pointed out. A month could be a lifetime out here in the arena, though.

"Yeah, and got you texting her non-stop whenever we're near a hotspot."

"Maybe she's his hotspot, ever think of that?" Mink quipped. He looked at the front of the room, and added, "At least she's normal, not like Miss Hutchens and Mrs. V-Z with their penchant to play with guns and take out gangs of thugs."

They had all agreed to call Jazz's wife, Mrs. V-Z. Verreau-Zerringue was just too big mouthful. BZVZ, actually. Because that GEM operative sure kept their other commander, Jazz Zerringue, on the move, hopping continents chasing her in between missions. He finally caught her, though, and they'd recently tied the knot. Their wedding had been a huge celebration—all the SEALs and even the admiral attended, not to mention Jazz's eight sisters and his best friend Hawk's large family.

Needless to say, the stooges had a good time. Lucas grinned, remembering all the fun chasing the sisters and partying all night.

Taken down. Damn. Dirk was right. His team was losing its bachelors one by one.

The large screen flickered for a few seconds and then Admiral Madison appeared. Everyone stood at attention. 'Mad Dog' Madison was Lucas' personal hero.

The man was a legend. Every young trooper had heard the story of young Lieutenant Mad Dog's heroic rescue in Operation Canyon Blitz of 4 SEALs, 3 army Rangers, 3 CIA operatives and 25 civilians who were cornered by the enemy, whenever war stories were brought up. Every Navy SEAL wanted to be like the young tough SEAL, Mad Dog Madison.

Now in his mid-fifties, the Admiral was well-respected by everyone, Army or Navy. War hero, famed combat commander, leader of the US Special Operations Command, good friend of the President, perhaps heading for the top seat of Supreme Commander.

Lucas stared up at his idol. Once upon a time, they even had a song about him to which to march. He still remembered mouthing the words while trying not to eat sand during BUD/s. He wondered whether his team mates had the lyrics in their heads after one of Mad Dog's pep talks.

We wanna be tough like Mad Dog Madison!
How tough is Mad Dog Madison?
He eats lightning and craps thunder
We wanna eat lightning and crap thunder
Just like Mad Dog Madison!

"At ease," Admiral Madison's smooth voice came through the speaker. "Congratulations on a successful mission, ladies and gentlemen. Good job."

"Thank you, sir," Hawk said.

"Our Joint Mission was a success because we all did our parts. Miss Hutchens' Intel about Yakob's involvement with sales of parts of the fallen Stealth has proven correct. And our inside man's tracking of Yakob's whereabouts was also important. Without them, our operation wouldn't have come about. Thank you, Miss Hutchens, thank you, Mr. Kingsley."

"My pleasure, Admiral," Amber said, "but everything depended on Shahrukh's being actually inside and pinpointing where the ceremony was being held. That made it easier since it saved the men valuable time. Your presence was mostly our good fortune, Shahrukh."

"Our operations crossed paths. It happens a lot these days," someone up front said. It was the man they'd "captured" along with the Cob. "Number Nine contacted me and I managed to stay longer. What with so many attending the ceremony, no one suspected."

"I appreciate COS' help. I hope your operation was just as successful?" Admiral Madison asked.

Shahrukh nodded. "Yes. With your taking me in as prisoner, there won't be any suspicions until I reappear again somewhere. By then, Number Nine should have taken care of some details."

Lucas had heard a bit about the COS commandos, of which there were nine, from conversations with Hawk and Jazz. Everything was hush-hush about them. Their orders were to not ask too many questions when other outfits were around, thus, curious as he was about the "crossed paths" component of the mountain search and seize mission, none of the SEALs nor he said anything. Their focus was on getting the Cob, anyhow. Now it was up to other people to question the prisoner and find out about the sold Stealth parts and the various terrorists organizations. Hopefully, the information would prove useful for their battle against the enemy.

Jazz reported the barebones details of what went down. He had a bird's eye view from the top of the wall before securing the front entrance for the SEALs' quick exit. The boat crew Chief gave his. Lucas took notes for future reference.

"Again, excellent job tonight. I'd like to hear questions from the rest of the men," Admiral said.

"Why is everyone calling it a ceremony and not a wedding, sir?" Joker asked.

"You should ask Cumber that question," Hawk replied.

Lucas looked up, surprised. "Me?"

"You and the stooges crashed through that barn door in such a timely manner, just as the whole thing was getting started, so I thought you'd know the reason," Hawk pointed out.

"Yeah, especially since you and the stooges knew part of the ceremony was to first roll around in bird poop before crashing through the barn door. Hell, you guys looked like zombies."

"Smelled like zombies too."

"Still do."

The place roared. Lucas shook his head and gave his buddies a side ways glance. They were never going to hear the end of this one.

"We are SEALs. We use all means," he deadpanned. "But, no, Joker, can't answer your question, but I suspected there was something odd going on, since you'd think they wouldn't hold a wedding outside an animal house."

"It's not a wedding," a quiet voice, with a slight French accent, interjected. Everyone turned to Mrs. V-Z. "It's a ceremony because a girl is being given away as part of an offering for some crime that had been committed towards Yakob's family, usually as a way to replace a dead relative. It's called *swara*. When Shahrukh reported back to Center about staying longer to help Admiral Madison out, he told T and the commandos about what was taking place and how he could be there without being noticed. T, of course, passed on the information to me."

Lucas had wondered about Vivi V-Z's role in the operation, but it was clear now she wasn't actually part of it at all. Vivi had a very, very soft spot for girls in trouble. She was currently in charge of some UN-funded organization for young women who had been victimized by international criminals, such as those who had escaped the sex trafficking cartels.

"That explains the young girl who climbed the rope," Zone said. "She sure made it up the wall like a champ."

"What happened to her?" Turner asked.

Zone shrugged. "Don't know. I pulled her up. She thanked me in English and she took off down the other side of the rope. I'd say she knew where she was going."

"That's my fault," Shahrukh said. "Once she told me she could climb very well, I told her the very moment there was trouble in the yard, to look in the direction where Team Alpha would be coming down. I advised her to wait till the men had climbed down before running there and scaling the wall. She was not to wait and explain anything to you guys because you would be busy and she needed to be out of sight of her immediate family."

"Thank you for taking care of her for me, Shahrukh," Vivi said.

"Our missions also crossed paths," Shahrukh said, with another small smile. "And T was persuasive, as usual."

All these crossed missions were giving Lucas a headache. That was the problem with joint missions. Everyone was busy taking care of their own agenda. All these people Mad Dog had brought in were mysterious as hell, always in some deep covert operation. Their last one big joint venture had the aforementioned T and Vivi running their own thing while his SEAL team had to explode a bridge.

A success, sure. But still, these women sure brought along a whole handful of other problems. For himself, he liked the KISS principle—keep it simple, stupid. As if reading his mind, Vivi V-Z looked in his direction, straight at him, a smile forming on her face.

"You must have taken a page from my tactical book, Cucumber. I had goats. Now I hear you attacked with chickens."

"Correction, madam, the stooges were wearing the chickens," Turner chimed in.

There were more chuckles.

"Lieutenant Commander Zeringue once told me, you do what you have to do," Vivi said. Her eyebrows came up. "Sometimes, simple things get the job done."

Lucas frowned. Damn if these GEM operatives couldn't read minds. Hawk had warned them they were trained in some kind of behavioral testing and manipulation or some such mumbo jumbo. It even had a name—NOPAIN—but he hadn't really paid much attention to remember what it was all about. He shuffled his feet and shrugged. Let's see whether he could read minds too and guess Mrs. V-Z's mission.

"I hope saving the girl who ran off would be just as simple for you, ma'am," he said.

Vivi shook her head. "Unfortunately, my job is a little bit more complicated since it involves women in a patriarchal-ruled region of the world." She sighed. "But you and the SEAL team gave me a good running start and for that, I thank you."

Bingo. He's got mind-reading skills too.

"Joint missions require clear communication," Admiral Madison said. His blue eyes flashed some emotion as he continued, "Remember our fallen brothers. They died because every damn agency wasn't sharing. Meanwhile, the rats stole our weaponry and secrets and sold them around the world. I'm here in DC still trying to untangle this damn mess. One thing is clear. I do not want a repeat of our men coming back in body bags because of greedy traitors. You have questions, go to your leader. They'll communicate your concerns to me. We'll try to double check all Intel through our joint missions. Are we clear?"

"Hooyah!"

Heard, understood, acknowledged. Everyone in the room was solemn as they remembered their fallen comrades. It had recently surfaced that traitor rats and sleeper agents had, for the last ten years, been infesting the CIA and FBI. It was going to take years to undo all the damage. The admiral had told them they were in the crossfire and all must be prepared at all times.

Lucas was up to the challenge. He had chosen to be a SEAL because, like his father, he wanted to serve and protect. All these joint missions might be confusing, but the admiral always laid out the big picture. He appreciated that most of all. What was important, what was the honorable thing to do, what was the stuff that made a warrior a warrior.

Hooyah! As always, he silently hummed the Admiral Madison song in his head.

* * *

Shahrukh liked this group of men and women. A bit too rowdy, compared to his smaller group of commandos, and yet, strangely, a bit too disciplined, what with their rules and standard operation procedures. But then, a military should be rigid, with obedient warriors who would act with courage, or everything would be chaos. If everyone started to question every order, there would be no action at all.

These SEALs in the war room were definitely warriors in his book. He'd seen them in action and admired the precision they had in executing their raid and capture of Yakob. Everything went smoothly, down to the last minute decision to have himself captured too, so that he would have a way out of there without drawing suspicion. They'd done so without asking questions and like good warriors, made a difficult mission seem easy.

On the other hand, these men would never fit in with his own covert group of commandos, better known as Viruses. A specially hand-picked nine, his unit had been trained to subvert and invade insidiously. After all, that was what COS Command stood for—Covert Subversive Command Center.

Shahrukh had no illusions about what his unit was. Their kind were silent killers. None of this "Hooyah" and "Yes, sir, yes!" stuff yelled out in unison. They were the shadows, the scary ones who could be monsters. Center had created them, experimenting more with some or, like with him, picking him for his vast knowledge of weaponry and poison. He was a relatively new addition to the Virus Project, brought in as a replacement for one of the few who had been murdered in a series of planned explosions. At first, he was "borrowed" from his former organization, but he'd chosen to stay on. He was intrigued by his new friends—this silent group of warriors who didn't quite own their own souls.

Of course he'd been intrigued. He had met his own kind.

Again, he studied those around him in silence. Their world was, by necessity, black and white. They functioned in direct action, looking for direct results. It wasn't a bad way to live, really. He imagined most civilized people liked to think the world moved that way. And young people, when they joined to be part of an army, should have this outlook—black was black, white was white. Simple.

If only.

With the meeting over, he should take his leave. He had much to do. He thought about the bag of opium seeds hidden away. He smiled, a small self-mocking lift of the lips. He didn't think these young warriors would like his next—very gray—move.

"Cumber, stay for a few minutes," he heard Hawk say.

The big guy from the back nodded. "Aye, sir."

A hand tapped him on the shoulder. He turned his attention to Vivi Verreau. Now, her kind, he was familiar with. GEM operatives were devious and worked in the shadows too, although Vivi Verreau, now married to that SEAL with the Cajun accent, were a lot less devious and secretive than her other sister GEM operatives.

"T wanted to make sure you have all you needed before you depart. What can I do to help?"

Shahrukh lifted his brows. "T must be worried. Or needing another favor."

Vivi smiled in acknowledgement. "You know T, always multi-tasking."

"Tell her this trader needs a good horse."

"I can arrange that. She also told me you might want to head to Karakoram and if you do, she'll need you to trade there for information."

Karakoram, the Silk Road. Everyone traded there, legally and illegally. Shahrukh had an idea what he'd be trading.

"All trade roads lead to Karakoram," he acknowledges. "It's very beautiful there. You should go sometime," he said. "You'll find certain vehicles full of girls who are sold as wives for desperate Indian families."

He understood the information Vivi was looking for. She had the biggest heart when it came to young women.

"I see." She handed him a card. "Call this number."

He took and pocketed it without reading it first. "I know T's busy running so many operations. I report back to Jed but from talking with the others, his head isn't one hundred percent in the game at the moment. Since I haven't seen him, I'd like T to tell me directly. She's better at analyzing the situation at Center than anyone else."

He wasn't really concerned about Number Nine yet, but it was always helpful to listen to outside opinion, especially from an expert people manipulator like T. If there was anything wrong with Jed, T would be the first to take charge of his current mission. He smiled slightly, thinking of another one of his Virus teammates, Number One, who had recently returned to the fold because of T. That had caused some friction. Perhaps he was wrong in his assumption on who would be in charge.

Nothing black and white. Nothing rigid. No standard operation procedure in his world of shadows.

"How many do you want me to purchase, Vivi?" Shahrukh asked. "You can't save all of them, you know."

"My husband once told me, we do what we can to save the world."

"Interesting. An old soul." Shahrukh gazed in Jazz Zeringue's direction.

As if he knew he was talked about, Jazz joined them. "Everything all right, *chou-chou*?"

"Yes. Can we get a horse for Shahrukh?" she asked.

"This late at night?" Jazz asked, amused. "What is this, a farm? Chickens, horses, goats. This is a war room."

"We have horses here. Our mountain guides are sleeping, though," Hawk, walking by with Cucumber, said.

"I'll have Lucas get you one after I've signed some papers. It'll take about half-an-hour, Mr. Kingsley."

"Call me Shahrukh. Thank you." Shahrukh turned to the big man who had been the brunt of most of the jokes. "That cut from the knife. Does it burn?"

Lucas shook his head. "Negative. I'm fine."

"Take care you let a medic take a look. We sometimes dip our blades in poison around here. I don't think you're in trouble but the knife might still have traces of poison to cause some infection."

Shahrukh studied the other men's reaction. Jazz and Hawk were looking at their man closely. Lucas Branson, after stiffening at the information, had released a breath and looked back at him calmly. Good man. Panic just made the poison, if there were any, work faster.

"I'll go get the horse. You go let Mink take a look ASAP, Cumber," Hawk ordered.

"I'm feeling fine," Lucas said.

"Better safe than sorry. ASAP, sailor."

"Aye, Sir."

Shahrukh didn't back down from the eye-to-eye challenge Lucas gave him. For a SEAL, he was a big guy. They were about the same height and Shahrukh was six feet three. He didn't think the other man had actually been poisoned but he wanted to test these SEALs, with their tough-guy reputation.

"You could have mentioned it after the Cob was marched off," Lucas challenged.

"It slipped my mind," Shahrukh said mildly. "I couldn't think properly with my ears ringing from all the gunfire."

It *had* been very noisy. They sure had used up a lot of ammo to capture one man. Such a strategy wasn't Shahrukh's style but he didn't run an army of men who had plenty of toys that went boom.

"Do you dip your blades in poison?" Lucas asked, looking him up and down.

"Sometimes," Shahrukh replied. "Nevertheless, there might be traces left on unclean blades. I assumed you've had your tetanus shots through the military."

Lucas nodded curtly. "Tetanus and other various shots."

"That's good. But like your commander says, better safe than sorry. If you feel anything unusual during the next forty-eight hours, report to your medic and get to a hospital."

"Right, in the middle of the mountains or jungles," Lucas replied dryly. "Just dial 9-1-1."

Shahrukh dipped his head in acknowledgement. "There is the possibility of your inability to get help while on a mission. Better stay on base."

"Fuck that."

"Branson," Hawk cut in, his tone quiet.

"I apologize," Lucas said curtly. "I'll take your suggestion under advisement."

Shahrukh nodded again. "Apology accepted. It was just conjecture. Probably nothing."

Deliberately, he caught Vivi's gaze long enough that she nodded imperceptibly. He was the foreign-looking entity in this room and probably not fully trusted. He didn't blame them. His file, if they had any dossier on him, probably wouldn't vouch for him being one hundred percent the good guy. But Vivi would make sure her husband kept an eye on the big SEAL.

Worrying about other people was the least of his concerns. He had his own duties to take care of and a few family obligations. He'd thought perhaps life would be easier if he put revenge out of his mind, that the past few years in his new environment with the COS commandos with their intensive experiments and mind subversive tactics, he would easily put away his former life. He had been wrong. Drugs and mind control experiments only worked in limited fashion. Unfortunately, his lifelong acquaintance with herbal drugs and poison had given him a certain level of immunity.

"I'll walk with you," Hawk said. "You can pick out the best available horse. Cumber, go to see the Medic. Mink! Go with Cucumber. I want a report of his status by morning, if not earlier."

"Aye, sir," Mink said, walking over, his gaze on Shahrukh. "What's the matter, dude? Feeling sick?"

"Nope," Lucas replied.

Shahrukh gave a slight smile. "Cucumber?" he repeated softly. Was that Lucas Branson's nickname? These guys were funny. "Is that what you're called?"

"To my friends, yes," Lucas replied tersely, his eyes narrowing. "Do they give out nicknames in your culture?"

"I have several, actually. Mostly, they're exaggerated promises, like Magnificent Bearer of Good News, a name I've yet to live up to."

"Huh. Well, there's nothing exaggerated about Lucas' nickname," the SEAL Hawk had called over, Mink, said. "Just a big promise."

Shahrukh noted the easy demeanor—intelligent eyes, friendly smile, alert stance. He suspected this one was the charmer of the group.

"That's good then," he said smoothly. "Cucurbitacin C, found in cucumber, can both be a toxin and an antidote to some poisons. I would say your nickname might be a lucky one."

Mink frowned, then shook his head bewilderedly. "Ohhhhkay. Let's go and let us check out that wound, bro. If we stand around here all night, I'll have to cucurbitacin somebody."

As the two men turned away, Shahrukh handed Lucas his card. "Here. My number. If you ever need any advice about poisons and weapons, feel free to call me."

"Uh. Thanks," the other man said, a puzzled look in his eyes.

He watched them walk off. It was an impulsive gesture but something told him this man and he would cross paths again in the future. After all, how could he ignore an old woman's prophesy which had sounded so crazy a decade ago but suddenly now came to mind, triggered, of all things, by a stupid American nickname?

To find your diamond, my child, three guides. In your dealings, be aware of toxins. In times of danger,

move like the spider. In your search, you must make
sure the cucumber flourishes.

His crazy grandmother, "seer" of his tribe, was long
gone, along with much of the tribal fortune. But her words,
seared in his memory, had surfaced with that silly
nickname.

"Ready?" Hawk asked, interrupting his reverie. He too
had a thoughtful look in his eyes.

"Of course," Shahrukh answered. Enough playing the
strange foreigner talking about poisons and potions. He'd
probably spooked half the people in this room. Back at
Center, he was known to be the quiet but mostly sane one.
Sully would probably have had a good laugh at seeing how
his attempt at small talk had devolved into too much
interest in another man's little flesh wound.

CHAPTER SEVEN

"Change of plans, Kit."

Kit looked up from the dictionary and translation she was trying to decipher. "Why?" She adjusted the mic in her ear. "What's wrong?"

They were in separate vehicles, getting ready equipment and notes before meeting with the girl. Sound checks, video feed, battery, foreign phrases, things like that. Then she and the female interpreter would put their head scarves on and make their way to the women's side of the camp to meet with the worker from Save The Children and the camp comptroller. Meanwhile, Sean and his photographer would walk around and take some photographs and interview those who ran the camp. Then once they'd gotten permission, they would meet at a public place to get few pictures of the girl.

The refugee camp was one of the poorest in the area, so they had prepared bags of clothing, food and toys as a gesture of goodwill. Kit was looking forward to finding out more about the displaced people here. Her research had shown Afghan refugees in Pakistan, especially around the borders, were the highest in the world. Yet, most media had only concentrated on the war and the politics, not on the plight of the homeless inhabitants here. Kit wanted to know more, first-hand.

"Minah is being sought by her relatives and she's in hiding. We can't interview her in the open," Sean told her.

"I thought she was getting help from a few of her relatives," Kit said.

"Yes, I thought so too, but according to the camp comptroller, things didn't go according to plan. A runaway from one camp to another was one thing, but a runaway from a *swara* while the ceremony was taking place is humiliation to her family. Everyone's out looking for her."

"Where is she?"

There was a pause. "Alone?"

Kit checked. "Yes."

"Take Joanna with you to the back of the camp," Sean instructed. "The comptroller sent someone to lead you to Minah. I'm on the other side of the camp and will come behind you with another guide. We have to take it slow and easy, as if nothing is wrong."

Kit pulled up her backpack from under the seat and began stuffing things she thought she might need. "We'll bring some of the gift bags to distribute. That way, it would look as if we were just moving among the women."

"Good idea." Sean said. Then, he added in a quiet voice. "Be careful, Kit. The comptroller warned that the relatives looking for her are armed."

A shiver of alarm went through her. "They aren't...going to hurt her, right?"

Another pause. "I don't know. You have to get that information about the groom before anything happens. Do you follow?"

Kit frowned. A young girl's life was hanging in the balance and all the man cared about was information about the groom? The guy the girl hated so much she was actually running away from him and his family?

She opened her mouth and then closed it. There was no time for debate right now. She had no idea what she was going to do but was determined to save Minah, wherever she was.

Joanna was also a seasoned photo-journalist, snapping pictures and making her way through the small crowd of women as Kit handed out the little bags. The ladies, some of whom spoke English, were gracious, thanking them for the packages. In spite of the need to hurry, Kit felt good at the small sparkle of delight she caught in the women's eyes when they looked inside their bags. There were even some squeals from the accompanying children when they saw the toys. Joanna recorded some of those moments with her digital camera.

One of the women tugged at Kit's sleeve, pointing in one direction. "There are some children over there, taking their lessons in the classroom. Perhaps you have more toys for them?"

Kit looked and saw that it was to the back of the camp, just as Sean had told her. Taking her cue, she smiled and nodded. "That would be great. Can you take us?" She picked up another box of goodies. "Let's go over there now, Joanna."

"All right," Joanna said, smiling down at the children. "See you later! I'll be back to show you some of these photos, okay?"

Waving at the others, they followed the woman. Kit tried not to appear to hurry too much, just in case someone was watching. She wasn't even sure what to expect, really. An *armed* family looking for one of its daughters was beyond any scope of her experience.

"This way," said their guide. "The children are anxious."

They stepped into a corridor along which were several open doors and Kit saw another woman's face peering out of one of them. Her blue head scarf was off, tied around her neck.

"That's Fatimah," their guide told them and waved. "*Assalamu alaikum was rahmantullah.*"

"*Wa alaikum assalaam,*" the other woman returned the greeting.

Kit had been practicing the two formal phrases, translated loosely as "Peace be with you and may Allah bless you" and "upon you be peace."

"*Assalamu alaikum,*" she said, a little hesitantly.

The other woman's serious expression broke into a welcoming smile. She returned the greeting softly and beckoned them to join her.

When Kit entered the room, she found it filled with young girls, probably between nine and fourteen, sitting quietly on the floor. They looked up at her expectantly.

Quietest classroom ever. Kit turned to their guide. "Can you introduce us and tell them that these bags are for them?"

"Yes. And while Fatimah is passing them out, you have to come with me."

"Of course." Kit turned and smiled at the girls sitting so sedately. "Hello, there!"

Joanna took a photo of them during the introduction. The girls' smiles of delight were worth everything. They were too well-behaved to rush to her, though, remaining seated and waiting for their teacher to give them permission.

At Fatimah's order, they all chorused, in English, "Thank you very much, Miss Kit and Miss Joanna."

While the teacher was passing out the presents, the guide tugged at Kit's sleeve again. Kit nodded and she and Joanna waved and walked out of the classroom.

"You never told me your name," Kit said.

"Hamidah."

"Thank you for doing this," Kit said.

The woman shook her head. "It's not my wish but she needs more help than I can give her."

She must be talking about Minah, the missing girl. Kit wondered how the women had gotten Minah here without everyone knowing. The girl's school was the perfect place to meet and her bringing the gifts certainly provided a way to tour the classrooms. Thank goodness for good ideas.

They entered a room in the back. A lone girl sat there, so still she could have been part of the furniture. Her head scarf was down too, revealing tumbled dark hair tied to the side, framing a small face. She stared at them, her features drawn in tense lines.

"You must hurry," Hamidah told them, and then addressed the girl sharply in Pashto, adding, in English, "I also told her to do the same. Minah, this is Miss Kit and Miss Joanna. I'll stand outside the door to make sure no one interrupts."

Joanna said something in Pashto which appeared to relax Minah into a shy and uneasy smile. Although she appeared uneasy, her dark eyes held a grim purpose. She said something back and Joanna indicated her camera and recorder. Kit recognized a few of the words. Reporters. Film.

Joanna beckoned to Kit. "She said she wants her story told before she dies."

Kit frowned. No one was going to die. Not on her watch. She had meant to start out gently, thinking she had to coax the details out of a girl who could hardly have had any experience about adult matters. The person sitting here, though, with that determined gaze, didn't need coaxing at all.

After a quick set up, Joanna indicated she had everything ready. Minah had been watching raptly. She leaned forward, as if eager to begin talking.

Kit pressed the record button. "She can tell her story in her own words," she said. In Pashto, she added, "Just start, Minah."

An avalanche of words tumbled out from the young girl's mouth

* * *

"Dude, I don't like how red that wound looks."

Lucas paused in the middle of putting on a clean pair of socks. "Stop looking at my body then. Besides, you're the one who sewed me. It's probably all red from your tugging that thread through my abs of steel."

Mink grinned and got off his bunk. He leaned down. "The stitches are beautiful. Like Picasso's work."

Lucas snorted and returned to his task. "Oh yeah, exactly like Picasso's."

Dirk's head appeared from the top bunk. "Have you actually looked at Picasso's paintings, man? Big headed, one-eyed, weird shit."

Mink reached out and touched Lucas' stitches. "Geniuses are never appreciated," he said absently. "Hmm. Soft."

"Hey, you're making me nervous," Lucas growled, elbowing him away. "And stop pulling on the stitches."

"I'm barely touching them. Heightened sensitivity. The bruising looks normal, though. Did you take the drugs the doc gave you?"

Lucas shrugged. "He said, if the pain was getting to me. It wasn't." It was just a knife wound. No big deal. He'd had injuries worse than this one. "Slept like a baby."

"Actually, you didn't," Dirk said. "I heard you tossing and turning quite a bit."

"Yup, me too," Mink agreed.

"What are you guys, my babysitters?" Lucas waved them away. "That Afghan insider's words got in your heads, clowns."

Mink pointed a finger at him. "I'm watching you closely today, pal. I know how you are. You'll fall over before you admit you're in pain."

Lucas got off the bunk. Mink knew him too damn well. "Yeah, yeah," he said nonchalantly. "I'm putting on some clothes and heading off to look for food. You two can squabble about who gets my big balls when I die from this little scratch."

He stalked off, feeling restless. He hadn't lied. He did sleep. Just not well. But he'd always had a difficult time going into full relaxed mode after a night of action so a bit of tossing and turning in bed didn't bother him one bit. It wasn't as if the bunk bed was as comfy as, say, Kit's bed.

Kit. Hmm. He was hungry for Kit. He wondered what she was doing right now. She did mention being out on an interview job where there were no hotspots for texting. Too bad. He had the sudden urge to ask her what her bed looked like.

He grinned. Now, he wouldn't mind having his abs and other body parts checked out by that woman. She had the most arousing way of smoothing her hands up and down his body. Half massage, half teasing promise. She had first done that to his back, from his shoulder blades all the way down his ass and over the back of his calves. Then, when he'd turned over at her soft request, she'd done the same to his front side, from his pecs, down his tightened ab muscles, over the top of his thighs...and then her mouth had come down between his thighs and...man, now that woman was Picasso with her mouth and tongue. Lucas growled again. Dammit, he was going to walk around with a telltale hard-on with two concerned bros at his heels.

Coffee. Lots of coffee and some protein. That was all he needed.

Fortunately, Dirk and Mink dropped the subject and went about like they normally did, bickering and talking about plans. There were a few other people eating with them and he chose to ignore the little digs about their adventure under the damned hen house. The moment the Stooges joined their table, a few of them started sniffing the air and plugging their noses, complaining about the odd stench.

One of the men clucked like a chicken and the others laughed.

"Pussies," he said mildly, as he started spooning food in his mouth.

Being alive was good. He could deal with a few good-natured ribbing from guys who had gone through a firefight with him, no problem. It was healthy just to let loose for a bit, even a few minutes, because too soon, one would be back on alert, taking care of the business of war. So he appreciated whatever time there was that gave these guys to hang and be human, and if it was his friends' and his balls they wanted to bust this morning, well, his were plenty big and they knew it.

"I'm still wondering about that strange dude with us at the end. You know who I mean," one of the men on the boat crew—Callahan—said, salting his food with the exuberance of a man who didn't think much about high blood pressure. "Wonder what else he gets out of it."

"What do you mean?" Lucas asked. "What are you doing, trying to ferment your breakfast?"

The other man grimaced. "Hey, just trying to make my food edible. Anyway, about that dude. You know how these double agents are. They don't do nothing for free."

"I don't think he's one, though," Mink said. "More like, undercover."

"Yeah, he seemed pretty calm through all that commotion on the boat, like he's familiar with big caliber guns shooting around him. I'm just curious, that's all. Not used to Joint Missions with so many different sides. Usually, we just pick you crazy SEALs up or drop you off, that's it. This time, we have to transport those female agents around too. Kind of effed up, if you ask me."

Lucas' ear pricked up. "Transporting them? Up and down the river?"

"Yeah, and at low speeds. They had their high-tech binoculars out looking for something or someone. Like I said, effed up."

This was all said quietly among them, since they were giving opinions about higher command. Lucas hadn't questioned the presence of Vivi and Amber, but he remembered how uncomfortable his team had been when they had their first Joint Mission experience with Vivi and her outfit. Not that they were women, because capable women in combat situations were fine with them, but because they were so damn secretive and no one appeared to know what they were up to. Hell, Vivi's role during their Joint Mission in Asia almost gave his two commanders simultaneous heart attacks when they found out. Too late, by then, of course, thanks to the wily woman who had known to keep her plans close to her chest until it was too late.

Lucas had admired the bold plan, though. Vivi had brought her A-game, letting the team do their job while she accomplished her mission. He liked her very much and she'd gained enough respect that neither he nor his team had even thought about what her role was in this particular mission. But, of course, the boat crew hadn't met her or Amber Hutchens before, and they were showing the same signs of uneasiness about working with strange people from outfits they'd never heard of.

Lucas thoughtfully studied the men as he chewed and swallowed his food. "Our team has worked with them. They're very capable," he finally said. "Whatever they're up to, they know what they're doing and won't jeopardize your lives unnecessarily. They aren't sight-seeing, I bet."

"I know they're scouting or looking for someone or something, but out in the open like that? Dangerous," Callahan said.

"Yeah, they're great looking women, but we aren't looking for hood ornaments for our boat," another of the guys chimed in.

Lucas grinned. Oh, man, Vivi V-Z and Amber Hutchens were going to have a fit if they knew they were being seen as hood ornaments. He felt compelled to defend them. It was his duty, since they were both, respectively, wife and fiancée of his commanders.

"One of them is actually an experienced tracker," he said. "She's probably looking for something that had to do with routes. As for the other, the first time I met her, she was disguised as an old lady and arresting military personnel left and right. I didn't even know that old lady was her when I met her again. Trust me, dudes. These women know what they're doing."

"Yeah," Mink agreed. "There are more of them too. All deadly, like Bond chicks. They all snare men like they snared our commanders."

The guys at their table snorted and laughed some more.

"If you're reporting back to your C.O.s, I've nothing against women in the military. These two, though, are more CIA-type, all close-mouthed about their agendas," Callahan said, "and you know how much they don't share."

Lucas nodded. CIA tactics had backfired before because of the agency's habit of not sharing vital information about their work at the most frustrating moments. "Agreed. All I can say is Admiral Madison is trying to change things by opening up different channels, using other networks. You guys know we lost some SEAL brothers precisely because of an operation that went FUBAR and it was all due to bad information, deliberately fed by rats in the CIA."

"Who doesn't know about it? The shit hit the fan last year and was all over the papers."

Lucas nodded again. He should know. He'd had a hand in the capture of Gorman, the traitor who had been selling secrets for ten years. There was a huge scandal in D.C. and heads were still rolling.

"Action speaks, right?" He asked. When the others nodded, he continued, "Then, look at what's happening. Mad Dog made a promise to get things done right. He'd gone to DC and headed up some independent hearing, spending all this time back home to get those bastards who are responsible for not just our brothers' lives, but so many others, by selling information and moving weapons to our enemies. Since he'd started pulling in these independent contractors and double checking information feeds, Mad Dog had scored us Dilaver, the main guy who had our SEALs killed. The Joint Mission netted us a kill and several important caches of weapons that had been missing from our storage facilities. Success and survival. That's all I care about, dudes. Fuck the paperwork and passing around of useless info."

"Hear, hear!"

"Amen."

"Seeing that you're tight with River Devil, and he speaks highly of you, I'll take your word about those indie contractors' capabilities," Callahan said with a smile. "I still can't see them jumping into the arena, weapons a-blazing, though, so can't even imagine how Mrs. Zeringue could have been with you guys during your stint in Asia, mowing down Triad brothers."

Lucas exchanged glances with Mink and Dirk. They were all remembering Vivi's herd of goats and how she had single-handedly divided a contingent of trucks in half for the SEAL team. They started chuckling.

"Callahan, you have to see it to believe it," he told the guys as he downed the last of his coffee. Pushing back his chair, he stood up. "I expect we'll be needing your assistance again soon."

"Yup. We'll get wet and party, as usual."

Lucas grinned. Damn river cowboys. They loved their boat and they loved to make a hell of a noise while in it. If he hadn't made it in BUD/s, he'd have tried to make it into the Special Warfare Combatant-Craft boat teams. An SWCC was in the league of Rangers, Green Beret and the SEALs, after all.

"Tell Devil to give me a buzz," he said.

"Gotcha."

Lucas, Dirk and Mink walked off, with Mink grabbing a handful of cookies and popping a couple into his mouth. The rest he put in his pocket.

"You'll just get cookie crumbles if you're keeping them for later," Lucas said.

"Oh, like it's going to be still there later," Dirk said. "Mink has the sweetest tooth this side of the world, man."

"Sweetest mouth," Mink corrected. "Sweetest tongue too, I've been told."

"Cumber's got the biggest balls. You've got the sweetest tongue. I must be the one with the longest dick."

Lucas snorted. "There, we're set to please all the ladies."

"Talking about ladies, you didn't sit in the corner passing love notes with Kit this morning. What's up with that?" Mink asked.

Lucas gave Mink a sideway glance. "Maybe you've got the nosiest nose."

Dirk threw back his head and laughed. "Maybe you should shut that sweet mouth or you'll also get the blackest eye."

Mink popped another cookie into his mouth, crunching it noisily. "Maybe you two are just jealous because I've got the nicest—Morning, Sir!"

They all stood at attention and saluted Lieutenant Commander Jazz Zeringue. He returned the salute. His wife, Vivi, was with him, dressed in camos.

"Good morning, Ma'am!"

"Stooges," he said, his grin betraying his amusement. "You know your voices carry down the hallway. I'm sure Vivi is thinking your looks are all you guys talk about."

"Our apologies, ma'am," Mink said.

"No need. We women enjoy your male banter," Vivi said, smiling.

"Going off already, Ma'am?" Lucas asked, eyeing the small suitcase Jazz was carrying.

"I have to pick up somebody and then I'm off."

"Last night's little melee brought out all the tribal family branches looking for that girl. Vivi wants to get to her before they do. I'd like the three of you to come with us. While she's doing her thing, I want you all to get to talk to some of the men there, see if you can get any info about the Cob's network. I'm going to talk to the *jirga*."

The *jirga* was the elected tribal heads. Getting on the *jirga's* good side was always the key to cooperation with the tribal families. Right now, they needed some of them to look away while they conducted some searches for the stolen Stealth parts.

"Aye, sir! We'll meet you outside with our gear."

CHAPTER EIGHT

Kit had done her research for their investigative report. Intellectually, she understood the concept of *swara*. In this part of the world, the Pashto people had a custom called *pashtunswali*—taking revenge to maintain honor. This was viewed as justice.

Their investigation into the Pashto singer's death report was based on the suspicion she was murdered because of this custom. She had publicly divorced her husband a year ago and went back into performing publicly, something deeply conservative Afghan and Pakistani men deemed as unseemly. Therefore her death came as no surprise to many people here. Although she was an immensely popular singer, the opinion that her murder was justified was accepted, with little moral outrage.

Sean Cortez had told her he wanted to dig deeper, to get the investigative piece to resonate about culture and deep tribal beliefs, and how change was difficult for Pashtun women. The topic was a timely one because of the recent push by Afghan and Iranian women for small changes, such as driving a car by themselves and even getting an education. Also, the one incident of the girl who had bravely fought against her elders because she wanted to go to school had made international headlines. Sean wanted to show more, to get the readers' imagination fired up about how these women were committing acts of bravery everyday by doing what would seem normal and mundane for those living outside this culture.

Kit was just as eager to use their Internet radio program as a platform for international women's issues and had studied her butt off on the subject. However, no amount of research prepared her for the words pouring out of Minah's mouth.

The girl looked so young. The matter-of-factness with which she told her story was chilling and disquieting. The first part was how she became a young bride. Her brother killed a rival family's son, whose father was also related to one of the tribal elders. The bad blood between the two clans escalated quickly. Finally, the other side demanded that his death must be avenged to stop more bloodshed. After the elders of her clan discussed among themselves, it was decided she was to be given as payment. She told Kit and Joanna that one day, when she was playing with her toys, her mother had sat down and told her she was going to be a bride of *swara*, as payment for her brother's crime. She was to be held in dishonor for the rest of her life and must prepare her life as someone on whom her new family would look down. For the rest of her life, she would be a reminder of the member who was lost and would be treated accordingly.

Minah stopped every minute or two so Joanna could make a quick interpretation and give Kit time to ask questions, but Kit found herself turning away to hide her tears. She felt so sad for the girl and helpless regarding her plight. Besides the interview, what could she do?

"What do you want to do now?" she asked, through Joanna.

The reply was quick. "Go to school, like Malala Yousafzai*. I want to drive a car." Minah patted her chest. "I want to be me."

Kit nodded. Such simple answers, yet so many obstacles. Her mind was working furiously, laying out any options for the young interviewee. Could she perhaps make her the focus of the article and get international attention for her plight, just like Malala? But it had to be done quickly because of her circumstances.

The laptop buzzed an incoming signal. Sean must be checking in. Joanna leaned over and clicked open a window on the screen. Sean's face appeared, slightly blurred from the bad lighting and odd angle from his tablet.

"I'm not too far away but the *jirga* is insisting I talk to them first. You need to ask about the husband or intended. Not sure whether they're formally married or not," he said.

"Okay," Kit said.

"I'll check in now and then. The *jirga*'s information is useful too."

He cut off before she could reply. She turned to Minah. "Your escape," she said, trying to lead the girl to the ceremony itself. "Tell me how it was possible. I'd imagine it must have been very difficult to run off."

"I thought so too, but it was actually quite easy," Minah told her. Her voice became excited, her gaze animated. "There was this man from the other family. Unlike the others, he was kind to me. He gave me something to eat, asked how I was. I told him I didn't want to be there because everyone hated me. I wanted my toys. I wanted books. He was very kind. He brought me a book and then he asked me how good I was at climbing ropes."

Kit frowned. "Why did he ask you that?"

Minah shrugged. "He came one more time after that and told me if I wanted to run, I must follow his instructions. He said, when things go crazy during the peace agreement ceremony, when my family and my...." She paused, looking away for an instant. Taking a deep breath, she continued, "When my family and the other family come together, there would be a lot of things happening. He asked me to keep looking at the wall to the back and when I see a rope coming down, I was to wait until the men climb down. Then when everything is happening, I can climb up and make my way down to this camp."

Kit and Joanna exchanged glances. "He gave you all these instructions," Kit reiterated. There was something more happening here than just a peace agreement between two tribal families. When the girl nodded, she asked, "What about the men climbing down from the wall? Were they your friends?"

The girl shrugged again.

When she didn't say anything, Kit tried a different question. "So, from your story, this man who helped you. Did he have a name? No? Okay. He obviously helped you, right? So what did these men do for you?"

"They were men with weapons. Many of them. There was a big fight. Bang! Bang, bang, bang! I wasn't afraid. I've heard guns go off before. My mother has shot guns before too. Big. Men. Big. Guns." She said the last four words in English and looked at them proudly.

Ah. There had been some kind of skirmish. "And they helped you run to the wall and you climbed it," Kit said.

Minah shook her head again. "No, they were fighting. I just ran. No one helped me." She paused, frowning, as if remembering something. "No, the man on top of the wall, he helped. He pulled me up. And he was a Westerner. Not local."

Whoa. Kit leaned forward. She glanced over at Joanna. "Ask her whether all the men who helped her were Westerners."

The girl nodded vigorously. "Yes, yes, they were Westerners. Dressed all in black, with black guns and face all streaked like fierce warriors. I don't know who they are but they were after some people. Not from *my* family." She said the last sentence firmly, as if to affirm she wasn't part of the other tribal group. She gripped her scarf nervously, tying and untying it. "Everyone is angry with me now. My own family, the teachers here, the *jirga*. They told me being disobedient like this is very bad and I bring shame to my family, running off. Is it wrong? Do you think everyone hates me?"

"Of course not. We don't hate you," Kit said. Haltingly, she pointed to herself and said in Pashto, "I will help."

Joanna turned to her sharply. "Don't make promises you can't keep. How are you going to help her?"

"International exposure. Something. We have to try, Joanna."

"Yeah, I know, but you can't tell her that. She's too young to understand how long that might take."

Minah grabbed her hand and said, in English, "Thank you. Want go school. Malala, my heroine."

She was nodding at Kit and Joanna, waiting for their confirmation that they understood her English and she beamed when they nodded back.

"Ask her where she can stay while we get help for her. I mean, her family is mad at her. What's her family name? And the other family too. We're going to have to make sure we don't accidentally talk to the wrong people."

Kit wrote down in her notebook. The names are all so long and difficult to remember. Malala, the girl about whom Minah was talking, was the name of the brave little girl who lived in the Swat Valley, who was shot because of her activism promoting education for women. Kit was now more than a little worried about the same fate happening to Minah.

She muttered to Joanne. "Back home, we're trying to get our girls to stay in school and not marry young. Over here, it's the complete opposite. They shoot at girls who want to go to school!"

"Education is dangerous, my friend. And an educated female is even more so," Joanna murmured back.

"I'm going to make that the headline of our piece," Kit told her.

The laptop screen came back to the live feed, with Sean's face peering in, his voice urgent. "Get out of there. Over. Get out of there, Kit. There are two vehicles heading your—fuck!"

There were some fuzzy images—houses shown sideways, running feet, scenery going by at odd angles—on the screen, like someone holding on to a moving cam and running. At the same time, Kit heard high-pitched voices out in front and the unmistakable squealing of tires. Then— a crash. People were shouting and screaming. Then, angry male voices.

They all jumped out of their seats. For one second, Kit stood there, her mind blank, indecisive.

Hamidah's head popped in, her eyes filled with fear. "They are here for her!" She pointed at Minah. "You have to go with them before they kill us all!"

Kit snatched up her laptop and backpack. She looked around her. There were no windows from which to climb out.

* * *

The moment Jazz made the turn and entered the refugee camp area, they all smelled it. The acrid smoky smell of burning. Something was on fire.

Everyone was running in one direction, pointing and shouting—men, women, children. Lucas hung his head out of the window, craning his neck to look beyond the gathering crowd.

"I suppose there's no fire department to call," he commented.

"We're supposed to meet with the comptroller at the office," Vivi said. "I'm sure no one is there right now."

"We'll follow the crowd but the vehicle is moving too slowly. Cumber, you guys get out and see what's going on. If it's a big fire, 'com' me. I'll radio for help.

* * *

"Is there a back door?" Kit asked, striding towards Hamidah.

"Yes," the woman replied. "In the kitchen."

"Kit grabbed Minah's hand. "Let's go!"

Once they were out of the classroom, the shouts were louder, followed by horrific crashes, as if people were kicking down doors and furniture. There were shrieks from the women and children. Kit recognized some of the words.

"Stop!"

"Help us!"

What was happening out front? Surely Minah's family wouldn't hurt innocent women and children.

The three of them rushed along, following Hamidah. There seemed to be an endless array of corridors leading to the back. Turning a corner, their flight came to an immediate halt. Black smoke wafted out of the doorway in front of them. The kitchen was on fire.

***

Lucas looked over the heads of the men in front of him and swore.

"That's the school," Lucas told Mink, lengthening his strides. "Radio back to Jazz. Tell them the school's on fire. I overheard Vivi saying the girl she's picking up is inside. Come on, let's get over there."

He pushed several onlookers out of the way. Some of the men were pulling out hoses. Others were standing in line with buckets.

As he ran nearer, he gave the surroundings a quick inspection. He didn't like what he was seeing. There was a big truck blocking the front of the school building. Another smaller truck had rammed through what looked like the remains of the entrance. A pile of wood was burning near the front steps, but that couldn't be what was causing so much panic among the screaming women.

As he reached the fence, the damage to it let him know it too had been rammed by something large—like a truck, for instance. And at the same instant, he saw the weapons in the men's hands.

"Mink," Lucas said, pulling his weapon out.

"I see them. Informing Jazz right now," Mink said, from behind him.

"Counted about ten. Three are defending the entrance. A few of them don't look Pashtun," Dirk observed. "They look...different. Body language is different."

"I say we go up there and make it three less," Lucas suggested. The people around him were already parting for them, as if asking them to do something.

"Jazz says fire truck is coming but it'll take a bit. It's at nearby village. Careful, though, bro. We don't want to cause an incident," Dirk said.

A shriek from behind interrupted them. A woman was running towards the school. "Oh, my daughter! My daughter's inside!"

There was a loud pop, then an explosion. Everyone, accustomed to sudden explosive devices, immediately jumped for cover. Lucas started running.

"That came from the school," he yelled over his shoulder. "I think that clarifies an incident is in progress."

* * *

Heart in mouth, Kit swerved around, pulling Minah along, with Joanna and Hamidah running behind them. Did the women use gas to cook in here?

"Run! We've got to get out of here."

"But the men in front!"

"There isn't any other way, Joanna! If they have gas back there—"

They retraced their steps. Hamidah was in hysterics, praying and sobbing. The smoke was already getting thicker and soon they would be choking on it if they didn't hurry. Kit grimly wondered whether she was going to make it out alive.

***

By the time Lucas reached the entrance, the small explosion had broken up the fight. One man was still valiantly struggling to get passed two others who were brandishing their weapons at him. Tall and tan, he didn't look Pakistani or local. Why weren't they firing their weapons?

Perhaps because there were too many women and children cowering behind overturned furniture and carts. Or perhaps they had a specific target. One of the attackers appeared to grow tired of just pushing back and went for his weapon slung over his shoulder. No time to figure things out too much. Lucas jumped into the fray.

Fighting hand-to-hand wasn't a problem for three SEALs but there was a disadvantage with the other party having the bigger weapons. This wasn't an ambush, though, and these men weren't acting as if they were here for battle. In fact, a few of them were just leaning against the truck, smoking cigarettes and watching the whole thing and not taking part in the melee. They seemed to be waiting.

Lucas couldn't worry about that. An explosion meant a fire and more explosions. He could put two and two together quickly enough. Obviously, they were after the runaway girl from last night, the one whom Vivi was intending to save, and—he winced as a punch connected with his stab wound. He turned and smashed a fist into his opponent's face.

Everything was happening very fast but in his mind's eye, he could see everything in slow motion. He caught glimpses of Mink and Dirk fighting back to back, punching and kicking. He knew they were running out of time because sooner or later these guys would change their minds about using their weapons and things would turn violent in a bad way.

Another small explosion rocked the building and the ground beneath their feet roiled like they were on deck in a bad storm, causing all of them to stumble about for a few seconds. Lucas fell against a pillar, his head making contact with something hard. He shook away the pain, looking about.

The whole place was a mess. He could see a pile of burnt paper in the smoldering fire that had first caught their attention. So that was what these fuckers were burning. Doors and planks lay around him, along with guys who had been thrown off their feet. The windows spat out smoke and dust. The men who had been throwing buckets of water through them had fallen onto their backs.

The small pause of inaction lasted only long enough before another set of loud female voices—he recognized English being spoken and Pashto—punctuated the air as well as sounds of some kind of struggle coming from within the building near the blown-out doors. Lucas steadied himself against the pillar.

He squinted his eyes as a group of people, all tangled together—arms, legs, hair—appeared. What the fuck—is that Kit?

CHAPTER NINE

Lucas gave himself a mental shake. If that wasn't Kit yelling and kicking at a Pakistani punk over there, he would eat his boot. There seemed to be a tug of war contest going on—a young girl in between Kit and the man.

"Kit!" Someone yelled, running into the fight. It was the man who had been trying to get by the two guarding the entrance.

"Sean! Help, don't let him take her!"

Everything happened at once. Lucas took a step forward. The punk hanging on to the young girl kicked out at Kit. The men who had been standing by the truck started spraying bullets. Everyone around dived for cover. Panicked screams. Running feet. Confusion everywhere.

Kit!

Uncaring about his safety, Lucas ran towards where the struggle had been, his eyes looking for Kit. She was on her knees, trying to get up, still yelling at the top of her voice.

"Stop those men! Stop! Sean, get off my legs!"

"Stay down, you idiot!" The man holding her down ordered angrily. "They're shooting at us."

"Let go! They're taking Minah away!"

Intent on getting to Kit, Lucas pushed some bodies standing in his way, watching as she got on her feet to run down the steps after the assailants. By the time he closed in on the half-toppled porch, she was fifteen feet away, running hard after the truck which had already begun to rumble off.

"Stop! Stop!"

Her voice, with that edge of desperation, cut at Lucas. "Kit!" he called out.

But she either didn't hear or she chose to ignore him. His heart dropped into his stomach when the sound of gunfire came from the departing vehicle. His idiot girl kept going, ignoring the splattering dust from the bullets hitting the ground. Apparently, these guys didn't want to kill anybody here, shooting at the dirt instead of people. But still, stray bullets could ricochet off anything and hit somebody. Kit didn't seem to care about that.

He had no choice. He had to run after her.

He took off without a backward glance. If Mink and Dirk were close by, they would have his back, taking charge until Jazz and Vivi arrived. He didn't think there was anyone to rescue back there. Whoever had started the fire—and he had a fair idea about their identities—had whom they were after and were getting out of the camp. Mink and Dirk just needed to get everyone to a safe distance from the school.

Ahead, Kit was yanking open the door to a van and sliding inside. Lucas sped up even more. The few seconds it took for her to turn on the engine gave him just enough time to reach the other side, pull the passenger door open, and jump in. She stepped on the accelerator and turned to him.

"Sean, we have to—" Her eyes rounded at the sight of him, her jaw dropping.

"Cupcake," Lucas said. He reached out and turned her face toward the windshield. "Keep your eyes on the road or you'll hit some kid."

There was a slight pause as she adjusted her speed. "Lucas? What are you doing here?"

"I can ask you the same thing but obviously you're in fucking disguise as Wonder Woman."

"What? What are you talking about?"

The truck ahead was heedlessly speeding off, not even honking at anyone in its way. People were jumping to the left and right to avoid being hit. At least that gave their vehicle some leeway to speed up too.

"Wonder Woman?" Kit repeated.

"Yeah, you think you can deflect bullets with your wrist bands? What the fuck were you thinking, running after that truck? Those guys have weapons, or haven't you noticed?"

The van bounced violently as it ran over a big rut in the road. Lucas put a hand on the dashboard to prevent his head from hitting the windshield.

"I don't know. They weren't shooting at me, anyhow. Just at the ground or in the air so people wouldn't interfere."

Lucas shook his head. "How do you know that? And what are you doing now?"

Kit gave him a brief glance. "Can't you tell? I'm chasing after the truck!"

"You have no plan!" Lucas yelled back. "What are you going to do, follow them home?"

In reply, Kit sped up, closing in on the truck ahead. They were out of the camp site and Lucas could see they were heading towards the mountain trails.

"If they're going into the mountains, they have to stop somewhere for horses," she told him stubbornly.

They were indeed making their way very quickly up the trails into the mountains.

"And then what? Are you going to ask them politely for the girl and have them nicely hand her over to you?' Lucas asked.

"I don't know! I needed to do something! What would you have done? Let them take her?"

"That's different."

"How's that?"

"I'm a man and I have weapons."

"Yeah, I'm a woman and I have weapons too. Big deal."

He felt like pulling his hair out. The woman had no concept of danger. She sped up even more as the truck ahead kept going at breakneck speed away from the village camp. Higher and higher they climbed. He had to stop her or they were really going to be out of reach, and they were only two against a truck of angry men. He was about to yell something caustic at her when his attention was diverted by the flap at the back of the truck opening up. A figure appeared. He steadied himself in the speeding vehicle as he adjusted a weapon held high against his body.

"Oh, fuck," Lucas said quietly.

It was unmistakable what it was. Lucas had carried one numerous times. A lightweight grenade launcher.

"RPG! RPG ahead!" Conditioned by his training, he yelled out. It was reflexive—usually, he had his team or a bunch of men around him who would be expecting shouts alerting them of danger ahead. He realized his mistake instantly, how useless his grim warning was. He was all alone with a civilian female. Kit wouldn't understand what to do next.

He reached out to grab the steering wheel, but found her shoulder instead. He turned his attention from the guy in the truck. Kit was leaning all the way forward, eyes staring straight ahead. The van's engine revved as she floored the accelerator.

"HOO-YAHHHhhhh!" she shouted at the top of her lungs.

Lucas stared at her, then grinned. Love sure had lousy timing. He turned back to face death instead.

They were so close he could see the tribal man's face broke out into a sneer as he took aim. Another stupid thought whooshed by in his head. *Death was coming fast and furious, baby.*

Smoke from the grenade leaving the launcher.

The longest second in his life went by.

Then, a horrendous crunch as metal met metal, a high-pitched grind as their speeding vehicle took the hit and their bodies absorbed the shock of the impact. He could hear the tires and brakes squealing as the vehicle swerved out of control. Kit swore a blue streak as she tried to get it back in control. They swayed from one side to the other, and he could have sworn the damn van was on two wheels at one point.

He gritted his teeth as they went airborne, then landed like a pile of junkyard metal back onto the road. The acrid smell of wires burning filled the air. The van careened out of control, finally coming to a grinding halt, facing the direction they'd just come from.

Silence.

Lucas found his hand still gripping Kit's shoulder. Hers were still clutching the wheel for dear life, her knuckles showing white. They were both panting hard, as if they had been running a marathon. His own heart thumped painfully against his chest and it took an effort to unclench his hand that was holding her so tightly.

He slowly, deliberately, wiped off the bead of sweat trickling down the side of his cheek with the back of his hand. "I'm thinking we didn't get killed with that hare-brained move."

The grenade did hit them. He *felt* it. Which made them sitting here, still in one piece, an impossibility.

"It worked." She turned. Her big smile would have lightened up a dark night. She put her arms around his neck. "It worked! It worked, it worked, it worked!"

"Stop bouncing the damn vehicle, babe. It's likely to explode," Lucas said. Much as he wanted to celebrate, there was still a grenade embedded in the van. "Let's get out...slowly."

When they stepped out to the front of the car, Lucas whistled. Half the small grenade was stuck right into the front grill.

"Fuck," was all he could say.

"It was a gamble," Kit breathed out. "He was high on a speeding truck and aiming down at us. If I drove the car near enough, the grenade wouldn't have the necessary rotations in the air to achieve its velocity. It would either bounce off us or..."

She waved at the sight of the grenade sticking out.

"How did you know what to do?" Lucas asked, a little awed at how calm she was.

"My brother is a fucking Airborne Ranger, that's how," she said, then broke into a laugh. "Listening to his buddies and him telling war stories paid off!"

Right in the middle of nowhere at the Pakistani-Afghan border, arms crossed, Lucas watched as Kit started to do a victory war dance, as if she'd just made a touch down in a game of football. She was covered in dirt from head to toe. There was a backpack half-hanging off her back. One shoe was gone, so the dance was actually sort of a limpy jiggle.

He was so going to marry this woman some day.

PART THREE

CHAPTER TEN

He looked yummy in uniform.

What a stupid thing to think about at this moment.

Kit couldn't help it. He looked so damn good—all big and tough, dirty and savage. That glint in his eyes that always made her imagine doing naughty things to his body. He was larger than live and she wanted to kiss him so badly.

She looked away, trying to gather her wayward thoughts. They had just witnessed a miracle. She shouldn't tempt fate twice and get distracted by her hormones. Hopefully, there would be time to do all that later. But right now, they had a problem. She looked in the driver's side window and retrieved her shoe.

"This thing is dead," she said, as they circled the damaged van. "I don't have my cell phone anymore. You?"

"Nope. But what I want to know is, how come you're here? I thought you were back home."

She still couldn't believe they had been texting each other in the same country. He must have some sort of secret program that gave a default location because whenever she tried to find out where he was texting from, it always gave the location as Langley. Yeah, right. She had so believed that. But still, she hadn't suspected he would be so close.

"I told you I was at work," she told him.

"As a public info officer, starting a new project."

"Yeah, well, this is the new project. I'm with a team interviewing female victims of the tribal warfare in this area." She stopped pacing and turned to look up the road. "We have to find a way to go after Minah. She's only thirteen and is being forced to marry some stupid warlord. Those men are from her tribe. The one who pulled her away from my arms was her brother. She told me when she caught sight of him."

It had been scary inside the smoke-filled building. She had been a lot more frightened in there than just now, in the truck. The smoke and ensuing panic were disorienting and it didn't help she was unfamiliar with her surroundings. And then Minah's relatives had shown up and went for them—well, Minah, really, but she wasn't going to give her up without a fight. That was a losing battle, though, with her holding on to a mere child while fighting off two big thugs. Joanna helped by smashing one of the guys on the head with a picture from the wall, but Hamidah and Minah were just too frightened to do anything.

"I see. My commander's wife was going to meet with her to help her."

Kit turned back in surprise. "What?" Minah never mentioned that. "Nobody said anything. I was under the impression she didn't have anyone to turn to."

What was a bunch of SEALs doing here picking up a young village kid, anyway? Minah mentioned a skirmish of some sort that had allowed her to escape. Were Lucas and his team involved?

"Don't know. We were heading to the comptroller's office when we smelled the fire and then heard all the commotion. Come on, let's get off the main road. I don't trust those guys not to turn their truck around. Let's walk down the road a bit."

"I can't leave this van. It has all my team's stuff in it. Equipment, maybe even important papers."

Lucas spread his arms. "We can't stay out here in the open. I'm in uniform and you're a lone female. We're in Taliban-controlled territory."

He was right, of course. If they were seen together by the wrong people, they would either be shot at or taken hostage. Kit looked at the van, trying to remember all the things she'd left inside.

"Well, at least let me gather stuff like passports and the weapons."

He cocked his head and gave her a long look. "Weapons. You have guns in there?"

Kit snorted. "Of course. Not big weapons. Just some stuff to defend ourselves with in case things get rough."

Lucas shook his head. "Cupcake, I don't think I like you at this job."

Kit opened the door of the van. "Oh, please, we're in Pakistan. Or Afghanistan, depending on which inch of dirt you happen to be standing on. They have border wars all the time. Do you want me to walk around without protection?"

"The point is, you shouldn't be walking around here at all."

Kit rolled her eyes. "What, you want me to walk around at home in the kitchen?"

"That's not what I'm saying."

She glared at him, her temper rising.

"Next you'd want me to wear a burqa and not show myself in public," she said. "That's precisely the male attitude that started this. Women are oppressed all over the world because men want to tell them where and when to walk, and marry."

All of Minah's words during the interview came back, refreshing all her previous feelings of anger and helplessness at the young girl's fate. Damn if she was going to let a man—even a hunk in uniform like Lucas Branson—tell her what to do.

"I don't need to deal with another male chauvinist pig," she told him. "Not at this moment."

* * *

Male chauvinist pig! What the hell! He was concerned about her safety. She was talking about taking up weapons and fighting fucking war-seasoned tribal lords who wouldn't think twice about blowing themselves and even their women up just to make a point.

"You're being unreasonable," Lucas said. "I'm not telling you about when and where to walk. Just not... here. It's dangerous here."

"To everyone!"

"Yes, but to women in particular. A lady can get herself killed running around *here*!"

She stopped stuffing her backpack. She took a deep breath, then straightened to her full height. She obviously thought that wasn't enough because she kicked over a small plastic stool that had fallen out of the van and stood up on it. Now they were almost at eye level.

"I'm going to cuss at you in very unladylike terms in a few seconds."

He grinned. "That's funny. Are you going to be carrying a stool around with you all the time so you can cuss at me to my face? You look cute when you're mad."

She leaned close. "One, you don't get to call me cute when I'm mad at you. Two, you don't get to order me around at all. I can fly off to wherever I want and you can't stop me."

Lucas frowned down at Kit. The woman just refused to be reasonable. "Oh, yeah?" Putting his hands on her waist, he lifted her off the stool a few inches. "Try flying now, Wonder Woman."

He'd expected her to kick out at him. Instead, she just lifted a dark brow. "Your big size doesn't intimidate me at all. I refuse to hurt you in the balls because I have use for them later."

He couldn't help but chuckle at that. She had a way of handling him that few did. She made him laugh.

"What am I going to do with you?" He wondered out loud. He still couldn't believe she was here, right in front of him.

"I have plenty of suggestions, but the most pressing one was to get important stuff out of the van and head downhill so we could get back to the camp."

She was right, of course. Why did women have a way of making things so complicated? Disappear into the trails, hike down the hill, get somewhere he could make contact with his team. Instead, he was out in broad daylight with a hard-on telling Wonder Woman what to do. Giving the surroundings a quick check, he lifted her up for a quick kiss before reluctantly setting her back on her feet.

"I'm sure my commander and teammates will be along once the fire and the crowd are under control. There can't be that many dirt roads off the main one. They'll take the one with the freshest tire marks or witnesses might tell them," he told her.

She licked her lips and smiled before turning back to the task at hand. He stood outside, keeping guard as well as watching her ass longingly as she crawled around the inside, pulling things out from under the seat pockets. He really, really wanted to just get into the van and close the door.

"Hopefully, Sean would follow them in his vehicle. Then we could get back here to unload the rest of the stuff before they disappear." She sighed. "I think that's all I can stuff into the backpack and this bag."

Lucas took the bag from her. "You purposely chose a pink one," he accused.

She grinned back mischievously. "Revenge is sweet, Cucumber dearest. I know how to deal with macho military men."

Lucas shook his head. Cucumber dearest. That had to be a first. She'd better not ever use that in front of the guys. Not that he could say that, or she probably would. He should have remembered, but things happened so fast just now, what with the fire, suddenly having Kit at his side, and not to mention, staring a grenade coming at one's face. Handling his sister taught him the first no-no thing about women was not to tell them to not do anything. Because they would go ahead and do it just to show you they could.

Damn, but he couldn't wait to show the guys the photo Kit took of that grenade inside the grill. Holy frog's hair, but that was close. He couldn't believe they had both lived to see another day. He glanced at the woman walking by his side. She was something else. Not one sign of stress on that pretty face at all. The guys would never believe what she did. He wished he could kiss her again—not a peck like just now, but a long, satisfying sensual exploration—just to convince himself all this was actually happening.

She looked at him. "What's the matter with you?"

"What do you mean?"

"You're staring at me and grabbing at your side like you have a stitch." She pointed. "Are you hurt?"

"Huh?" He looked down. Sure enough, he'd unconsciously been pressing his hand to his side. He turned it over. "What the..."

"You're bleeding!" She exclaimed, coming to a stop. "I can't tell with all the stains on you. Are you badly injured?"

"I'm fine," he told her. He frowned at the dampness in his hand. "The stitches must have broken, that's all."

His wound ached a little, just a slight cramp. He hadn't even noticed it until now.

"Stitches? What happened?"

Lucas shrugged. "Just a little cut. Let's walk on. It's really no big deal."

Her eyes narrowed suspiciously. "A cut from what? Did one of the tribal men slash you last night when you raided their peace offering ceremony?"

He stopped walking and grabbed her elbow. "How the hell did you know what happened?" he demanded.

She wrinkled her nose. "I'm an investigative reporter. I know these things."

"You don't know anything." He shook her arm. "Not a damn thing gets out in print or media, you hear me?"

She frowned. "I can't promise that."

"Kit, I'm serious here. You can't report that. Stick to your women's right stuff, but leave our raid out of it."

"How am I going to do that? It's part of the story of how she escaped," she pointed out.

Lucas was at a loss for words. This was serious, but how could he explain to her without revealing more information? He'd never been any good at expressing himself in a diplomatic way.

"You can't write about it and not expect consequences," he said.

"Wait a minute. Are you threatening me?"

"Of course not. But I don't want the raid out as public news. It could jeopardize our other missions. Do you want that to happen?"

There was a pause as they trod on. He glanced over hopefully. She was biting her lower lip, her expression serious.

Finally, she spoke up. "As an army brat, I know how important this is for you, but as a reporter, I can't just shut up about it, Lucas. Do you understand what I'm saying? It's my job to investigate and report the facts." She put up a hand when he tried to interrupt. "Wait, let me finish. It doesn't mean I'm not on your side. It doesn't mean I won't be careful with my reporting, but if what your team did save this girl's life, I can't just ignore that."

"Of course you can," Lucas said, exasperated. "Just omit it."

"I could, but even if I do what you ask, my immediate boss might not. He's going to listen to the audio file of my interview with Minah, you know. And the interpreter was there with me. Do you expect her to keep quiet too? Lucas, it's not possible."

He stared ahead. There was a bad feeling expanding in his gut and it wasn't his stab wound bothering him either.

"Your boss, is it this Sean fella you keep asking about? Is that the guy fighting with the men outside the building?"

"Yes," Kit replied.

"Well, maybe I can have a talk with him."

That made her turn her head. "Oh, no, you don't! You're not going to have a talk with Sean about what to or not to report!"

"Why not? Man-to-man, maybe he'll understand."

Lucas realized his mistake immediately. There was a fire in her eyes that would probably burn him into dust if it were real. Damn him and his big mouth. He'd just committed the second no-no crime.

"Man-to-man?" She repeated, a dangerous undertone in her voice.

He let out a long sigh. "Okay, that came out wrong." *Say it, Cumber, say it. No one but Kit to hear it.* "I'm sorry." He'd been reduced to apologizing for saying what was on his mind. Forcefully, he added. "But I still think you're...inappropriate...to reveal my team being here. Or any special ops, for that matter."

She gave him a terse look for a moment, then walked off ahead of him. He studied her stiff shoulders, which started shaking. As if...

"Hey, are you laughing at me?" With a few long strides, he caught up. Oh yes, she was trying not to laugh out loud. "What's so funny?"

She gave up and chuckles bubbled out of her. "Oh, my God. You're so funny when you try to be nice and not cuss. Inappropriate," she mimicked his look of disgust at having to apologize. "You sounded like Miss Clementine!"

Lucas gave her another pained look. "Look at what you've done to me. Next I'll be wearing pearls and chasing you around in a pink...condom."

She choked, her mirthful glance accusing. "Take that back! You're just trying to get back into my good graces."

"Who's talking like Aunt Clementine now?" he mocked, then affected his aunt's Southern accent. "Get back into my good graces, you bad, bad boy!"

Lucas breathed a quiet sigh of relief. When one couldn't win with words, one could always fight back with humor.

* * *

Kit was glad Lucas changed the subject, as they continued their way downhill at the side of the dusty "road." It was an easy guess and he'd all but confirmed she'd been correct. She didn't want to argue with him, not about this, anyway. The thing was, she could see why he would be concerned. Navy SEALs did a lot of secret missions and some of them not koshered. If this was one of them, her reporting it could get his team in trouble.

One problem at a time. Her main thing now was to get back to her team and figure out how to reach Minah. She glanced at Lucas and frowned. He looked and acted okay but his breathing was ragged, as if he was a tad out of breath. There was no way he was tired. She'd seen him throw furniture around like they were toys without even breaking into a sweat. That sheen of perspiration on his face right now—was it from the afternoon heat or something else? She looked down at the stain near his waist. How injured was he?

"They should be looking for us by now," she said.

He squinted at the distance. "Yeah. Maybe there were some injured people and they're helping to get them out of the way. There were many children milling around, but they're pretty hardened, even for kids. Fire and men shooting weapons hardly faze them."

"That's sad. Those men should be punished for burning a school. They didn't even care that there were people inside!"

Lucas grimaced. "You're lucky they decided not to shoot. Their objective was to get the girl, but you're right, those guys have very little respect for females in school. They see it as a revolt against their wishes, you know. Those girls and their parents have my respect. The Taliban thugs have been known to throw acid at girls walking home from school as a deterrent."

"That's insane!" She shook her head, horrified at a sudden thought. "We have to hurry back. I'm even more worried about Minah now."

She felt stupid for not having thought ahead. She'd prepared for everything—how to dress and behave, bringing the gifts, practicing some Pashto, researching on the custom of *pashtunwali*. Why hadn't she thought about the possibility of the young girl's relatives suddenly appearing? By the time that realization came, it was too late.

Although Lucas didn't say anything, she knew he was thinking the same thing, though. How were they going to get to the girl in time?

"I hear a vehicle coming," Lucas said quietly. The sound of its engine echoed through the mountainous terrain. "Not going to be here for another five or ten minutes, though. There are no footpaths, nowhere to hide."

"Okay," Kit replied wrapping her head scarf more securely. She slowed down her gait and let Lucas stay in front of her.

"Been reading up on the customs around here," he said, approvingly.

"Don't get used to it," she warned. Over here, women walked behind the men. Intellectually, she accepted the cultural differences, but it was still tough emotionally. She had seen it with her own eyes how, when they'd first landed in Karachi, the men leered at women who were alone, sometimes walking very closely to make her uncomfortable. They would even peer into any cars that had a lone woman in it, as if they had a right to check her out. Sean had told her they didn't do that so much in Mingora, the capital of Swat Valley, where they'd been heading, where women were more traditional.

Lucas gave a low chuckle. "Trust me, Cupcake, I'd rather be behind you watching your pretty ass."

Her first glimpse of women walking around covered from head-to-toe, with the magnificent mountains as a backdrop, was a cultural shock. How on earth did they not trip over, carrying children and shopping bags, and not being able to see? And yet they looked perfectly natural, walking around in the fields or following their male relatives if they were out in town.

"I really hope it's either your men or my team," she said, looking at his back.

There was already a slight change in his demeanor. Straighter stance. Bigger presence. So damn male, even while carrying her pink bag.

CHAPTER ELEVEN

Shahrukh read the instructions from T's note, which Vivi Verreau had passed on after the meeting in the US war room. Out of habit, he stroked his chin as he considered his options. The beard had to go soon. The merchants he was meeting at Karakoram wouldn't be expecting a dirty mountain gun-slinging insurgent-type buyer. For some reason, they expected those men to want the bigger things, not the small sophisticated item in their possession.

He leaned back against the brocade pillow and took a sip of the coffee set on the low table next to him. He savored its strong, pungent taste, took a deep breath and closed his eyes briefly. A few hours' sleep would be nice.

"Tired?" A woman's voice floated from the direction of the door.

Shahrukh opened his eyes. He studied the figure at the entrance. "You look so docile, so traditional, Zerya." he finally remarked, replying in the same Kurdish dialect she used. "Maybe time can change a person."

She smiled and she suddenly looked the same, in spite of those world-weary eyes. "That's funny coming from a man who is looking more like his Kurdish self than the usual suave New York image he's adopted." She came closer, the bangles on her wrists and ankles tinkling. "Yet, I know you haven't changed. Still looking for broken pieces of treasure. Still playing the game, I bet."

Shahrukh shrugged. He hadn't been in "The Game" for a few years now. There was no harm in letting Zerya think he was still with the treasure hunting organization. His "new" life with the commandos at Command Center the last few years had been even more secretive than when he was one of those working for The Temple.

"Life is a game," he said.

Zerya shook her head. "No, it is not. But we forgive you, since you've been brought up by frivolous Western ideals. Your adoptive parents have taken your soul away from the Kurd people."

Shahrukh laughed. He'd heard that line so many times since his teenage years when he was "returned" to his people, it no longer hurt him. He had nothing to prove any more, except maybe to keep a promise to an old woman.

"All Kurds away from Kurdistan have lost a little of their souls," he agreed in his usual non-committal fashion when dealing with family matters. "As have you. Being among a smattering of Kurds while surrounded by Pathans is hardly your style."

"Is that the reason for your visit, then, Rukh? Just curious why an old lover is hidden away here?"

Shahrukh leaned back further into soft backrest, contemplating the woman standing so serenely. There was a time he'd been in love with Zerya. She was everything he wasn't—absolutely sure of her place in the world and intensely dedicated to family and honor. He was the total opposite, feeling out of place among his own people and not as sure about his place in a family who had lost him in a war, and now that they'd found him, demanded things from him he didn't understand. Growing up with his adoptive parents, he'd wanted brothers and sisters with whom to play and quarrel. Then, fate had given him back his lost family and he'd returned—with the blessings of his parents—and he'd found himself among brothers and sisters with whom he'd no emotional attachment. Zerya, the neighbor's daughter, had been the only one who understood him. Or, so he'd thought.

She casually sat down, leaning over to refill his cup. "Or maybe," she continued softly, switching to speaking French-accented English, "you're, as usual, looking for other people's treasure instead of your own?"

Shahrukh smiled. "Sharp as ever," he said, in English. "Always using everything as a weapon. I half-expect you to be carrying a machine gun under that skirt. Tell me, why aren't you in Paris with the rest of your unit of *Peshmerga* fighters?"

Warrior blood flowed in generations of Kurds. The Kurd Resistance allowed women to join their ranks and as a people, they'd been at war for centuries, fighting for a land for their people. *Peshmerga*—those who confront death—was the fighting force beloved by the people and feared by the enemies.

"The CIA has informed us there was danger ahead, that some leaders are targeted for assassination. I was one of the few ordered by my superiors to disappear for a while." Her voice held a trace of bitterness. "So, here I am, in the middle of nowhere, unable to do much but...entertain."

"Liar," Shahrukh softly chided back.

She cocked an eyebrow at him, relaxing further into her seat as she bit into a pomegranate. "This is Afghanistan. As a woman, all I can do is stay inside here and be protected. What else could I be doing?"

"Documenting pieces of a Stealth airplane that is being slowly dismantled, perhaps? Trying to either sell or buy parts in the great bazaar of Karakoram, perhaps?" Shahrukh asked.

She slowly chewed the fruit, licking the juice on her shapely lips. Her almond-shaped eyes held amusement as she searched his for clues. "Ah. The downed Stealth at the border. Like I've asked before, why do you keep going after someone else's treasure and yet never profit from it? All those treasure hunters you work with, aimlessly running around picking things up and exchanging information—do you ever want to use them for yourselves? Or your people?"

And there lay the core of contention between his old lover and him. She was all about their people and fighting for land. It was something noble, a way of life to which their clan was dedicated. He'd not lived up to her dreams of being a clan elder's son, one who would pick up the mantle of blood and glory for revenge and justice.

"Actually, I have," Shahrukh said. "I used The Temple's many treasure quests as a way to look for the lost diamond."

"Bah. You listened to your grandmother's silly stories about diamonds and maps instead doing something tangible." Zerya sighed then propped her head up with a hand. "Quests. Those people call it "The Game." You joined a bunch of mercenaries who called themselves treasure hunters, looking for antiquities for collectors. Life, death, and honor, Rukh. No game in those three things."

He couldn't blame her for sneering at his former job. It wasn't quite as shallow for him. The Temple had roots with an ancient tradition that went as far back as the Kurds; in fact, their histories were intertwined and that was one of the reasons Shahrukh had joined them. Surely, with all the treasure quests these people were looking for, they would have some clues to help him find his diamond.

But he wasn't here to explain about history and the Templar Knights to Zerya. Explaining that it was his way of returning honor to his family and clan would be a waste of time. Zerya never believed his grandmother's stories, anyhow. And if she ever found out he was actually now part of the US government, she would probably see it as a betrayal.

"Treasure is all about value," he said. "It's my quest to find what is of value to me, hence my way of life."

"And Stealth parts are valuable to you, how?" Zerya asked, amused again.

"Not all its parts. I want to know the name of the seller to look for a certain part."

After Shahrukh had reached the site and given the mortally wounded pilot a password, the dying man had imparted a secret with his last breath. There was a special missile on board, painted with a newly-designed cloaking paint that made it untraceable to radar. That was the weapon he needed to find.

"Is that why you were seen with Yakob?" Her smile was sweet. "Don't worry. No one but us knows you're anything but an ordinary Pathan trader."

Spies. Everywhere. He wondered whether she knew Yakob had been detained and perhaps was now trying to negotiate his freedom by giving back some of the parts he'd stolen or bought. Everything technological taken from the Stealth, big or small, was worth something in the market and everyone wanted to make a profit. Some for revenge. And yes, some for honor.

"Yes," Shahrukh replied easily. "He told me he was going to buy it at Karakoram. You have the name of the seller and I need it."

Zerya leaned over and placed a hand on his thigh. Her kohled eyes gleamed with feminine invitation. "And what do you have for me and my freedom fighters?"

* * *

Lucas scanned the area. They weren't exactly in the danger zone but it was the Afghan-Pakistan border, where the situation was nebulous. If he was right, they were close to the crossroads, where everyone with vehicles had to travel through, from mountain passes to the cities, and vice-versa. On any given mile, one might bump into Pakistani border troops, Afghan soldiers, tribal warlords who had been de facto rulers in these mountainous regions for centuries, and freedom fighters from various factions, all moving around traveling merchants, refugees, herders and border farmers.

This was, in his opinion, the most eff'ed up place in the world, with a people living on two sides of a border trying to survive. They had been doing it for thousands of years, it seemed. Why not another thousand? He'd been in the military most of his life, so warfare was nothing new, but he did feel for the normal, everyday folks who had to go through their daily lives facing possible bombs from any and every side.

A truck with a cloud of dust behind it came into view. He motioned to Kit to stay off the trail and stick by the thick bushes. If they were Pakistani soldiers, they would leave an American soldier alone. Certain tribal militia would most likely pass by without more than a glance because they had made agreements with some of the US commanders who had visited them. There would also be the assumption he was probably not alone, which was a good thing.

The truck slowed down as they came nearer. The dust made the sunlight hazy as it floated all around them. A figure jumped off the truck and started charging, screaming an almighty war cry.

"Get down!" Lucas shouted back at Kit, hoping she was already hiding somewhere.

If these people had wanted to kill him, they would have shot him already. He crouched lower, waiting for the running man, and slowly straightened up in surprise as the dust settled and the running figure loomed larger…, or actually, smaller. It was a child coming full speed at him and it wasn't a war cry. It was more like, "Yah! Yah! Yah!"

A woman screamed. Then another figure jumped off the back of the truck.

"Daner! Daner!"

There was an urgent stream of Pashto and some other language Lucas didn't recognize but since the man was unarmed, he stayed where he was. No sudden moves to panic anyone in the truck.

The kid stopped a few feet away and his big green eyes stared up at him.

"Meri-kan!" He yelled at the top of his voice. "Meri-kan! Meri-kan!"

"Hey, hey, no shooting. Friends! Friends!" The man coming after boy finally reached them and scooped the boy into his arms. He looked at Lucas apologetically and said, in a heavy accent, "Sorry! He's just boy. Play with soldiers, always stupid. Sorry!"

The boy's expression was earnest. He made the sign of a gun with his forefinger and thumb. "Bang! Bang! Me-rikan! Me-rikan dead!"

The adult said something sharply at him but the boy was obstinate, repeating his phrase.

"Sorry! We go now!" The man backed away.

Lucas frowned. "Hey, wait. What language did you just speak?"

The man just shook his head, while continuing to back away. "We mean no harm. We are from small tribe and my son, he is too friendly with soldiers." He paused, looking behind Lucas. "But you better go fast. It's not safe for you and the woman. Taliban behind us."

The boy started struggling. "Taliban! Bang! Bang! Me-rikan dead!"

"Wait! Why does he keep saying Me-rikan dead?"

The man shook his head again. "He's a boy. Nonsense, you know? Go now. We all have to go!" Then he added in Pashto, *"God be with you."*

As the man hurried back to the waiting truck, the boy looked over his father's shoulder and pointed his "gun" at him again. His green eyes were fierce.

"Bang! Bang! Taliban! Forty-mike-mike! Me-rikan dead!" He covered both his ears as if he was hearing something, then shouted back in perfect American English, as if he'd heard the phrase hundreds of times, "You tell Me-rikan, ack-ack, bang bang!"

Lucas stiffened. What the— Those were military slang words! "Hey! Hey!" He yelled.

The man turned his head and spat. His expression was just as fierce as the child. His English came out in staccato notes. "You stay away! Go back to your friends! Taliban coming, you understand? You cannot save my son. Get lost! Bastard!"

The man threw his son into the arms of a waiting woman in the back of the truck and hauled himself up. Seeing the boy starting his struggles afresh, Lucas kept coming after them. The woman was talking in a stream of urgent sentences to the child, her tone full of admonishment. The truck started rumbling off again. The little boy shook his head and looked back at Lucas, his expression obstinate and determined.

"Tell Meri-kan! Ninety-nine! Incoming! Incoming! Boom! Ack-Ack! Alpha Mike Foxtrot! Ack-ack! Seventy-Fiff!"

Unable to catch up, Lucas stood there listening as the sound of the boy's voice became further and further away, still shouting military terms over and over at him. "Incoming! FPF! Tell Meri-kan! MIA! The Unit! Seventy-Fiff! FPF! FPF! Where in world is Raven? The Unit!"

He cursed out aloud in frustration. He should have been able to catch up with that fucking truck. That kid was trying to tell him something, he was sure of that. He impatiently wiped off the sweat dripping into his eyes with his sleeve. Fucking damn it. He couldn't even keep up with a fucking—

"Lucas!"

He took deep breath. He'd forgotten Kit was all by herself. Cursing again, he turned around and strode back to her.

"You were supposed to be in hiding," he said shortly.

"I was but I came out when I saw the kid," Kit said. She frowned. "Why are you so angry?"

"Because it could have been a kid with a weapon. Or an explosive device. You have to listen to orders, Kit!"

"I was listening to orders. I only came out when I was quite sure he wasn't going to blow you up."

Lucas continued shouting, "That man coming over could have started shooting. Anything could have happened. The people in the vehicle—"

"I assessed the situation before I came out from behind the bush," Kit cut in, very quietly. "And you're still shouting at me. Stop it. Why the hell are you so angry?"

"Because the kid was trying to tell me something and I can't...catch...a damn truck." Lucas leaned forward, putting his hands on his thighs. "I'm fucking out of breath. What the hell—I'm fucking out. Of. Breath."

"Lucas? Lucas!"

* * *

Kit ran to Lucas when he fell on his hands and knees. She watched in horror as he started retching.

"Lucas!"

"I'm okay. Turn around. Don't loo—" The rest of his words were expurgated in a series of horrible retching noises.

She ignored his hand trying to push her away and squatted down beside him. His face had a greenish hue. He thumped a fist against his chest, as if he needed to dislodge something. Then he leaned further forward and vomited.

Ugh. Kit had to look away for a moment. She stood up to take off and unzip her back pack, pulling out a bottle of water. Unscrewing the cap, she put it in front of his face. He snatched it from her and put his lips on the mouth, sucking down the liquid like a man dying of thirst.

"Slow down! You'll puke it all out again!" Kit punched the muscular arm to get his attention. "Slow down!"

His head was tilted back, exposing his brown throat, and she noticed for the first time he was perspiring profusely. Even his hair looked damp. Something was definitely wrong.

When he was done with the bottle, it fell to the ground. He leaned forward, putting his hands back on the ground. His eyes were closed. He was still panting, his breathing erratic.

"Lucas?" She squatted down again. "What's wrong?"

"I'm okay," he said again. Then determinedly, he repeated, "I'm okay."

"Fuck your okay shit, Lucas Branson. You just vomited a pile of yellow blob in front of me. You tell me what's wrong with you right now or I'll kick your ass all the way down this mountain."

Her threat brought a tiny lift to his lips. He took a few deep breaths. "Let's get off the road first." He slowly stood up, as if assessing his condition. "Behind that bush again, Kit. I don't think those people were speeding away from us."

She nodded. "Come on." She slipped under his armpit. "You're swaying, so don't say you're okay. Lean on me. Walk!"

"I'm not leaning on you," he said firmly, unhooking his arm from around her shoulders. "I can walk to that bush. No problem."

Frustrated, she let him do it. She had had plenty of experience with macho males who refused to admit they needed help. When her father broke his leg, he'd acted exactly the same way. She watched as he carefully made his way to the nearby shrub, his gait stiff and measured.

"Yeah, sure you can, Frankenstein," she muttered.

She made a face at the puddle of puke on the ground before following Lucas to the small area behind the shrub. With the heat coming on, it was good to be in the shade. She was worried at how much Lucas was perspiring. At this rate, he was going to be dehydrated in no time.

"I want you to drink more water," she told him, crisply, as she rummaged in her backpack. "Here's some mouthwash too, if you want to gargle."

"I don't need—"

He stopped in mid-sentence when she spun around and glared at him. Eyes narrowing, he took the mouthwash, obediently gargled and spat to one side. When she continued to stare him down, he took the small bottle of water and took a swallow from it.

"You aren't well. I don't want to hear your protests. Your face tells it all, mister," she said, keeping her voice as matter-of-fact as possible. "So, we have to come up with a plan."

He growled something back under his breath. His face told her it was probably something with some curses and he just didn't want her to hear the words

"Yeah, yeah," she said, rolling her eyes. "Me scared of Big Baby. We'll rest five. You tell me what you're feeling or I won't budge for ten minutes."

"I'd rather talk about that boy and that truck. They're running from someone and we need to prepare for those people coming behind them."

She nodded. She understood what he was implying but nothing was going to matter if he couldn't walk straight, much less defend them from any coming danger. "That too. But first things first. Come on, time's a-wasting."

He gave a grunt of frustration. "I must have eaten something bad this morning," he said and gave a shrug. "When you travel as much as I do, the tummy often doesn't agree with the food."

Kit frowned. "If you have food poisoning, then you're going to be weak and dehydrated. You're also perspiring a lot."

Lucas impatiently wiped his forehead and studied the wet patch on his sleeve. "Yeah," he said, sounding surprised. "I'll keep drinking liquids, okay? But right now, if those people are really being chased by Taliban insurgents, we have trouble ahead. They're going to see our van and if they stop to investigate and see any signs that we weren't captured, they might decide to backtrack to look for us."

"I took everything of value I could think of," she told him. "Passports, licenses, the tablets, cash, weapons—"

Lucas shook his head. "Weapons! Why are they in the damned bag? We need them where we can easily access them."

"Relax, babe, they're in my backpack side pocket. See?" She showed him. "They aren't powerful toys like yours but they'll have to do."

She handed the 9mm to him. He checked it and then gave it back to her. "I'm assuming you know how to use it," he said.

She nodded. "Pretty good, but only target shooting."

"Okay, but in a firefight, there is no controlled environment. They're shooting back at you, so you won't be thinking calmly about which part of your target to aim. Got that?"

She nodded again. It seemed so strange to be calmly having a conversation about shooting someone. "Are we...really...going to be in a firefight?"

He touched her lower lip with his forefinger and smiled. "In spite of your Wonder Woman status, I'm hoping to avoid that. I have my .45," he said, "but ammo is low. If there is a firefight, we're toast. All we can do is be prepared. The first thing is not to walk down the road until they pass us. Damn it, I wish we had some way to get hold of my team."

"What do you think they're doing now?" She asked.

"Hawk would take the team down to the camp once he knows there had been an altercation. There are several scenarios. If the fire was serious, Jazz, Mink and Dirk would be helping to put it out until the firefighters show up. They might leave then and come looking for us, which would be good. But there are several forks through the mountain borders. Unless he gets some help from people who saw us, he won't have a chance guessing and will try to get Hawk to get some air support to see if they can find our vehicle or that other truck."

"My team will come looking for me too," Kit said. Sean would be worried about everything in the vehicle and want to retrieve them. "Surely they'll search one route while your team goes the other."

"Yeah. And they both might be searching the wrong routes while we're here trapped with the Pakistani Taliban. It's crazy in these mountains, babe. Everyone is fighting everyone. Who knows why they're after that kid and his people, but what that kid was yelling to us was all military slang, like he had a message."

"Lucas, he's only a kid. Maybe he picked up the terms at camp and was just running through them because he saw a soldier in uniform." She'd to admit the kid was scary intense with the delivery, though. "Just a thought."

"But there was no doubt they were deathly afraid of their pursuers. Who are coming this way." Lucas slumped against the tree, holding his stomach. "Fucking hell."

Kit moved towards him, only to be pushed away by a big hand. He turned and disappeared into the thicker side of the bush. She shuddered at the horrible sounds of vomiting, followed by sharp, deep breaths, like a man trying to get air.

"Lucas?"

"Yeah. I'll be out there in a sec."

She lifted her head, listening. "I hear rumbling."

His breathing was quieter. "I hear it too. Stay...where you...are."

"Are you okay?" Stupid question. He obviously wasn't and of course he was going to say he was fine.

As predicted, he said, "I'm fine." He sounded hoarse, as if he was having difficulty moving and talking at the same time. "Stay where...you are. I can see...the road from where I am. We'll know soon...whether it's just another vehicle or...something else."

Kit didn't like way Lucas was talking so haltingly. She tried to look through the branches but the shrub was very thick. The partial gap she found gave a bird's eye view of the road in front. The vehicle coming whooshed into view and was gone before she actually saw anything other than the fact that it was one of those huge SUV-like vehicles and there were two men hunched over the top with weapons. As soon as it went by, she made her way carefully into the darkened area Lucas had slipped into. It smelled acrid and she had to pinch her nose to stop from gagging. Then she saw him, slumped against a tree in a weird position. She suddenly realized he was unconscious and hurriedly stumbled towards him.

His face felt fiery. "Lucas!" She lightly swatted him on the cheek. "Lucas!"

No response. He was much too big for her to even attempt to move. She had to get him up and about. Uncapping the bottle of water she had in her hand, she poured it over his face and bent down.

She needed to do something. She couldn't let her fear for Lucas win over logic. There had to be a way. Closing her eyes, she channeled her father, the drill sergeant, and shouted, "Cucumber! Get on your feet, you lazy bag of bones! Why are you lying on your back? Get up! Get up before I put my boot so far up in your ass we'll both end up in the hospital! Cucumber! Up on your feet and attention! What fucking kind of SEAL are you, anyway?"

She almost fell on her back when Lucas flipped over and jumped to his feet. He saluted and yelled back, "Standing and ready, Sir! We are standing and ready SEALs, sir!"

She didn't know what SEAL team he was on, so she just made it up, substituting her father's Airborne unit, "Hey SEALs from left to right, Hey SEALs, we're out of sight, we're trained to fight, we're trained to kill, if you can't do it, we damned sure will! Motivation, dedication, graduation, teamwork! Left! Right! Left, left, right!"

To her relief, her on-the-spot cadence worked. Lucas started—she wouldn't call it marching—putting one leg forward and then, the other. But he was following her lead back out into the open air, where she could at least check on his status.

"Come on, soldier, left, left, left, right, left! I don't know but I've been told! Green grasshopper has a red asshole! One, two," she sang, still channeling her father, "sound off, three, four, sound off, one-two, three-four!"

"Who the hell taught you that?" Lucas asked.

She glanced back at him. His face was pale and his eyes were intently on her feet, as if he needed to follow her footsteps.

"No, don't answer me," he continued, "And don't break out into any fucking Airborne Ranger cadences. I'll vomit again. Violently."

"Hey, army brat, you know. My dad's a drill sergeant and boy, did he know how to get my brothers and me out of bed. Well, not with the bad language, of course. That came from hanging around army folks too much." She stopped at a spot that was still shady but was a bit higher than the previous one. "You're going to sit here and drink more liquids while I climb this tree."

He frowned. "Why? Are you planning to hide us there if those guys decide to backtrack? Because we're going to need a hiding place. I counted eight of them in that ATV, maybe nine. At least four were carrying machine guns."

She swallowed and tried not to show her fear. "You saw all that and fainted from fright?" she quipped.

He grinned. Her heart did a slow somersault. He managed to look sexy-hot even though he still seemed ready to fall over any second.

"Smart-ass," he said. "I was so unfazed by those guys, I decided to take a nap, that's all. But some loud howling about a boot up my ass woke me up. That kind of threat usually gets a man's attention, you know."

Kit felt her face heating up. She did yell out some horrible threats, all courtesy of watching and listening to her brothers beating each other up.

"Did its job," she said. "I'm climbing up the tree to see where we are. I have a tourist map in my backpack—"

"We aren't going on a scenic tour, Cupcake," Lucas cut in. "We need to get out of here."

She shook her head. "Will you let me finish? I have a map that someone local has marked for me all the places to avoid. I remember he mentioned caves that have been abandoned by the Taliban that were near the camps. If I can see one of the tourist landmarks from up high, I can figure out how close we are to them."

He stared at her for a moment. "There's nothing to see up there but more trees and the main road," he told her.

"I know, but I've also done research on the web. Aerial research because I enjoyed the view of the Swat Valley rivers. I bet, if I can figure out where the river is, I'll recognize a few things I've looked at from those aerial views. Then I can locate them on the tourist map and we can...oh, will you just let me do this? It's going to take them half an hour to reach our van and if they stop to search...we have just enough time. Okay?"

He sighed. "Go ahead. I'll just lean against this tree and hold it up."

She grinned at him. Freaking macho man wouldn't admit it, but she wasn't going to let him know she suspected he was having a hard time standing on his feet right now. "Don't...take a nap while I'm up there. That's an order, sailor," she said.

She pulled off her skirt. His dark eyes narrowed at sight of the pair of tight boxers underneath.

"Don't worry," he murmured. "Those legs have my full attention."

CHAPTER TWELVE

SNAFU. Situation all fucked up. Lucas looked at the pair of luscious legs climbing above him. Long, silky legs. Toned and tanned. Attached to a pair of pink boxer thingies that clung to hips and other female parts. SNAFU turning rapidly into FUBAR.

He banged his head against the tree. What the hell was he thinking, letting her climb up a tree, her ass all but naked, in the middle of the freaking Afghan-Pakistan disputed war zone? He must be out of his fucking mind.

He looked up again and caught a glimpse of Kit's ass as she wriggled through a tight spot. He closed his eyes for a second. He was letting that woman get away with every hare-brained idea without even putting up a fight.

And his food poisoning excuse was only half the problem. He knew full well something was fucking up his system and bad food wasn't the cause. He rubbed the area where he'd been stabbed the night before. It was radiating heat while the rest of his body felt icy cold.

His whole head hurt as if something was eating his brains out. He tapped his forehead against the tree trunk again. He could not afford to lose focus. He couldn't believe he fainted. Fucking hell. He was leaning against the damn tree for support. He straightened up stiffly, using one hand to steady himself.

Kit was right. They needed to get to some sort of shelter before he lost all ability to protect her. Then what? He shook his head, trying to clear the cobwebs.

If those fuckers stopped to check the van—and they would because of the grenade—it wouldn't take them long to make some educated guesses about who had been in the vehicle. He'd glanced around while helping Kit pack. There were tons of clues they'd left behind. English-language newspapers. Music CDs. Articles of clothing. Kit said she'd gathered most of the important stuff in her bag, but still, in their hurry, they could have left something.

He nudged the small pink suitcase with the toe of his boot. He frowned, trying to remember whether Kit climbed the tree with her backpack on her. She did, didn't she? Why didn't she leave it down here with him? Granted, it wasn't a huge sack, but it would certainly impede her movement. And if she slipped.... He looked around for it. Nowhere in sight. Damn it.

Cucumber, you've got to start thinking ahead or you're going to get both your sorry ass and hers killed.

He was the experienced one here. She was counting on him to get them back to that camp. He had to stay vigilant, have eyes on the back of his head. Kit had never been in this country, where everything could blow up at any second, where there were so many factions fighting one could end up making the fatal mistake of helping the wrong side. Like that truck being chased. Who was that kid and why did he yell out those odd messages that most American troopers would understand? Was he just crazy from this sickness or did he hear some kind of warning in that boy's voice? And why the hell was the Taliban chasing after them if the kid was just mouthing nonsense?

He needed to try to decipher the words and see if they made sense. This fucking pounding in his head wasn't helping. He slammed the side of his fist against the tree trunk in frustration. *Think hard, you jackass. Anticipate ten steps ahead. Act towards goal.*

One thing was for sure. Kit and he couldn't walk down the main road. He was sure his team was out looking for them already so it was just a matter of staying safe until they saw Jazz's truck. Or maybe they'd radioed in for choppers, especially if they'd taken the wrong route and couldn't find them. Of course, they wouldn't know the two of them were now on foot. Their first assumption would be that he and Kit were still going up into the mountains.

He frowned. No, surely his team would also know, sooner or later those assholes would shoot at the van to stop them from following. Maybe they'd expected him to turn around and so they were waiting down there. Except they knew Kit was the one who had been driving.

His gut tightened from nausea. Unless he stopped feeling like this, it was best to get them out of the main road and just sit and wait. He would just be a liability to Kit.

Kit. His little Drill Sergeant Cupcake, leading a pussy asswipe who couldn't stop puking his guts out because of some damn infection.

Now she wanted to head to the caves. He knew about them, the abandoned ones by enemy insurgents after a crushing defeat by Pakistani and US forces. They were put under surveillance by the local government for a while but that was two years ago. He knew the local government troops weren't that vigilant, so that area wouldn't be one hundred percent secure. But there could be some kind of way of communication there, if they were nearby. That was the problem—he had no idea how far away they were. It wasn't a bad idea, except Kit thought she could find them. By climbing up a tree. In her boxer panties.

He groaned out loud.

This was so, so fucked up.

* * *

Shahrukh studied the cloudless sky. The mountain view was spectacular today and from this privately-hewn ledge, he could see for miles. Some of Zerya's Kurd guards had recognized him and given him a lot of freedom to roam here. To them, he was still one of the chosen sons of the famous elder who had won all those glorious battles for them. His father was descended from royal blood and had expected Shahrukh to carry on, even though, as a youth, he'd never even known what life outside the United States was when he came to live with his people.

Shahrukh nodded at the guard and waved him away. The other man disappeared into the background without a word. He gave a small reluctant smile at how quickly his wishes were obeyed among relative strangers. Just because they saw him as something akin to their leader. Just because his father's legendary exploits gave them the impression his lost son would have the same qualities and the same inclinations. Even though he'd been gone for a few years, the oral tradition of passing down history and bloodlines made it impossible to be invisible among his own tribe. They knew of him and would treat him accordingly.

He took out his small satellite phone, turning the switch from cell to satellite signal. In these mountainous regions, where quick communication was impossible, it was probably one of his most valuable assets. His was issued by his agency, specially built to look inconspicuous, with an ability to scramble signals as well as other special capabilities. Here, in the hidden caves near the beautiful Swat Valley, using the device to talk about secret operations, special weapons and government agents made him feel like he was Batman. Amusement bloomed and the corner of his lips reluctantly lifted. Prince Batman. He'd have to request that as his code name when he returned to Center. So much more cool-sounding than boring Number Four.

"T," he said, without any greeting.

"I've been waiting for your call." The feminine voice at the other end came in clearly, velvety and sultry, like its owner.

"How did you know I would call you and not Number Nine?" he asked.

"It's my job to anticipate everyone's moves," she replied. "And you call because you need him for a task but needed confirmation from me about his state of mind."

As usual, the woman was perceptive. Everyone at Center had been watching his unit's main man very closely. After all, the infamous Ice Man was showing *emotion*.

"I heard there was a violent fight between him and One. First, who won? Second, can Nine handle any assignments?"

Number One was Alex Diamond. If Jed couldn't perform, Shahrukh would report to him instead of Number Nine, even though what he needed done needed the latter's expert touch. But Diamond had just returned from his self-imposed sabbatical and although he liked the man, Shahrukh didn't know him that well.

"I wouldn't call it a violent fight, darling, but yes, your concern is valid. As far as I can tell, Jed is handling everything normally." There was a slight pause. "Perhaps a job taking him away from here would be good. He's stalking the Medic floor like a wild animal and that only makes the staff nervous."

Jed stalking. Jed in love. The very notion made Shahrukh smile again. Jed in love and stalking the Medic Center for updates on his lover were definitely interesting developments he wished he could witness for himself.

"Have you ever heard of the parable of the old lone wolf who found his life mate?" he asked, amused.

There was a tinkle of laughter. "No, but I hope it has a happy ending and the mate doesn't die because if that happens, said lone wolf is going to be a dangerous lone wolf."

"Oh, indeed," Shahrukh agreed. He glanced down at the scenery below and added, "Is he dangerous?"

"Darling, he always is. Now, if you mean whether he's in control of his emotional well-being to cancel someone for you, yes, I believe you should get him out of here for a while. I have too many stalking men around here at Center and not enough whips."

T was the current operations chief for the mission. No doubt she had her hands full dealing with Jed and Alex Diamond at each other's throats, what with Helen injured in Medic. He hoped she would make it. But these matters weren't his top priority right now. His mind turned to his own operation at hand.

"I located the dealer in Karakoram. I had to exchange a favor," he told her. Several, actually, but those were personal ones. "I need Jed to meet me to cancel a target."

There was a small pause. "We don't actually lend our operatives out for target cancellation, Number Four," T finally said, her voice a little cooler. "There are certain rules by which we must abide. Center is not a Dial-An-Assassin service."

He wanted to point out the experiments the nine commandos went through were called the Virus Project for a reason. They were all assassins functioning from within a cell, structured to destroy elements one by one. But it wasn't in his nature to argue about semantics.

"Just get Jed here and he can decide," he said, in his most reasonable voice. "I'm sure in the end, there'll be a connection to some government sanctioned mission one way or another."

There was another soft laugh at the other end. "You know that kind of manipulation doesn't work with me, Rukh."

His senses rang out a warning at the sound of his name. T was about to make her mental sniper move.

"I'll give Jed your message but I think you need to take care of some business first," she said.

Here it comes. "What is it?"

"Vivi called and told me the girl you helped has been caught by her family. I need you to use your negotiation skills to find out where they have her. Now, a family blood feud isn't going to be settled by money. I'm sure your Kurd familial connection has some weapons to be a little bit more persuasive, Rukh."

Bullseye. T knew about the Kurd weapons. Shahrukh breathed out a quiet sigh. "The Kurdish battles have nothing to do with this war, T," he said.

"Perhaps not directly, but you're asking *me* to make a government connection, remember? We can't interfere in a local blood feud now that the SEAL team has achieved their objective, which was capturing the Kob. But if your...contacts...would release the weapons they've taken from the caves when the insurgents ran off, now all targeted parties would listen and negotiate and we have a—how did you word it—sanctioned government mission."

She had the exact reasonable tone he'd been using earlier. He could only admire the intelligence behind the tactic, how she struck a deal without his actually agreeing to it. NOPAIN, her GEM organization called this technique. Nonverbal Persuasion and Innovative Negotiation. Not having been long with Center, he had yet to master this art of war. One day, perhaps.

"And what will my contacts and their group get in return?"

"Shahrukh, they're female *Peshmergas*. Our GEM operative in France has access to certain information and people, and thus can help find out who is targeting the top female leaders. I'm sure your contacts will be interested."

He might as well admit defeat before he gave away even more. "I should just leave the wolves in your care," Shahrukh remarked. "They could fight to the death while you claim a bloodless victory."

T's soft laughter made him smile in spite of the enormous responsibility she'd put on his shoulders. He supposed he deserved it. After all, he'd asked for a life to be ended.

"Rukh," she said, "I must find some fun in my situation any way I can. Jed will get hold of you. Talk to you soon."

* * *

"They're tracking us. I can feel it."

Kit glanced behind them. They'd been moving steadily down the mountain but now that they were off the main trail, their speed was impeded by foliage, rocks and detours.

"How do you know?"

"I can feel it in my guts."

"You puked them all out already," Kit quipped, "so you must be wrong."

He was perspiring so much, she was worried he wouldn't make it. He hadn't talked a lot, trekking without giving away his obvious discomfort, only stopping to heave that awful noise, which he tried to muffle with a wad of clothing. He needed to sit down and rest, but his paranoia of being followed pushed them along.

"Come on, lift them feet, left, left, left, right, left," Kit urged. "We're not far from that back entrance, according to my map."

"If your map is right," Lucas muttered.

Kit hoped so too. Where else could they go? The main road was unsafe in his condition. The river was too far away and, according to him, had numerous tribal route lookouts. At least the caves were either going to be guarded by some government militia or abandoned, so it would be an ideal place for Lucas to sit in while she continued down to get help. She'd purposely kept that last part of her plan out of their discussion, of course. He would never agree to it and she didn't want to argue while they were heading there. He would see soon enough that she was right.

The local guide she'd talked to had told her he'd once worked as an interpreter for the US army, going out with different outfits to communicate with tribal chiefs and villagers. Of course, when he recognized the division her brother was in, they'd quickly become friends and he was more open, telling her about different adventures. Sean had listened in with interest and later told her she was an asset to her crew because of her way of getting people to talk and do things for her.

She checked on Lucas again, who continued to be strangely obedient. When they were moving furniture at Miss Clementine's, he was the one directing them all and refusing to budge when the girls insisted on moving some heavier items themselves. This quiet and submissive side, going left when she said left, even allowing her to climb the tree when he'd have done it if he were himself, was how she knew the big guy was suffering.

He caught her gaze and his mouth lifted at one corner. "Don't worry, Cupcake. I'm keeping guard from the rear."

His voice was hoarse. She frowned, inspecting him closer.

"We're almost there," she told him.

They walked around a large rock formation with shrubs and suddenly there was a clearing. She stopped short and stared. The "cave" was nothing more than a hole on the side of the mountain, covered with some dense shrubs.

"It's manmade," Lucas told her quietly. "It's the back end of the main caves. An escape tunnel, dug in a maze inside, I bet. I've heard about it from other units. Who told you about this again?"

Kit looked at the large hole again. She didn't mind the dark or even the idea of rodents, but crawling through tight spaces underneath the earth wasn't quite how she envisioned a cave.

"Some guide who used to work with the units," she replied. "He didn't say anything about it being just a big hole. I mean, a cave is...you know..." She opened her arms wide, and added, with a shudder, "He told me the insurgents hid in these places, hiding for days. How is that possible?"

"They probably lead to bigger caverns inside. An escape tunnel like this has advantages." Lucas rubbed his chin. "This being the back end, it would eventually lead to the front. We can crawl our way inside and see if we can find our way out on the other side. That way we can do what those who escaped did, skipping the main route when it wasn't safe for them."

"But if our side's looking for us, they wouldn't know we're in there," Kit said, kicking at an exposed root. "I mean, they're probably heading for the front side."

"How do you know that?" Lucas asked. He dragged a branch that was in the way of the tunnel's mouth, then swore softly, holding his side.

Kit knew he was getting weaker. He was pulling at the limb with both hands. "Let's rest a bit, then..."

"No. We're going inside ASAP. But first you tell me how you know they're looking for us at the caves." He narrowed his eyes. "You did something else up that tree."

Kit nodded. I spray-painted my scarf."

He stared at her. "What?"

"You mentioned they would be sending out the choppers sooner or later and that little kid shouting all those acronyms gave me an idea. I spray-painted it with BOLOCAVE. I figure Mink would know it means "be on look out for cave" and it's just logical to assume I'd mean nearby caves, which would be these here, except I meant the other side." Kit sighed. "I hate small dark spaces. Why are you looking at me like that?"

He was giving her that dark intense look that always made her heart do crazy somersaults. If he didn't look so ill, she would have certainly considered doing naughty things to that sexy body.

"Because you're the most awesome of camping companions. Spray paint." He gave her a tired grin. "What the hell do you have in that backpack anyway?"

"Emergency stuff." Wait, what did he call her? "Did you say I was awesome?"

"Yeah. The most awesomest of cupcakes," he answered softly. "I wish we were somewhere else and I could do the stuff I always do to sweet cupcakes."

Her heart bounced from the pit of her stomach, did three flips, and landed somewhere in her loins. Or at least, it felt that way. "In that case we'd better get going and be rescued," she said. She pulled out a flash light from her back pack. "Tada! That will at least make it less scary crawling in there. But I'm going to be holding on to your pant leg all the way in, if you don't mind."

Lucas picked up the bag. "A fine sight Mink's going to see at the other side. A puking SEAL with a pink bag dragging a claustrophobic woman hanging on to his leg."

* * *

149

The last time Lucas felt this weak was when he contracted influenza in college that progressed into pneumonia, which had landed him in the hospital. It was so bad, he'd withdrawn for the rest of the semester. He remembered having no strength to perform the simplest tasks.

Right now, he had no feeling in his legs and it took all his concentration to go down on all fours to start crawling into the hole in the ground. From the look on Kit's face, she was worried about him as well as afraid at the idea of going inside the ground. For her sake, he must stay strong and effective. He had to stay prepared. His SEAL training had given him the ability to draw on his reserves and conceal this wretched nausea and pain from her as much as possible.

He was so proud of her quick thinking and bravery he wanted to kiss her, but he doubted she would want that from someone with a bad case of puke breath, even though he'd dutifully used her mouthwash. But damn, the woman turned him on even when he was almost out of man juice.

He could feel her hold on his ankle tightening as they went in deeper, leaving the sunlight behind them. It was very dark and he waited till his eyes adjusted before continuing. The small flashlight illuminated enough that he could see the hole widening ahead. There were probably roomier caverns beyond that.

"Are you all right?" he asked.

Her breathing was erratic. "No," she said, in a very tight tone of voice. Her grip was a vice. "I'm trying not to scream."

"I'm right here," he said.

"Okay."

They went further for another minute.

"Lucas, I can't breathe. I'm going to...to...."

He was too big to turn around to comfort her. They couldn't afford her losing it right now. He must somehow distract her before her fear took a stranglehold.

"Kit! Listen to me. Are you listening?"

"Y...yes..."

"Remember you were leading the way and singing cadences?"

"Uh-huh."

"I'm going to sing and you'll repeat my lines after me, okay? Do you hear me, Cupcake?" He changed his tone of voice to more matter-of-fact.

"O...kay," she said, her voice a little higher than usual.

"Right. I'm moving forward, right leg, then left, and I'll sing a line. I expect you to repeat. You copy that?"

"Yes." Her breathing was shallow but she sounded more in control.

As they made a slow progress toward the widened area, Lucas started to sing, waiting for her to follow before continuing: To his relief, after starting in a breathless, squeaky tone, her voice became stronger with each line. His own crackly voice came out like someone who had been smoking six packs a day.

Chant-singing his favorite song made him feel stronger. He repeated the refrain:

"*We wanna be tough like Mad Dog Madison!*
How tough is Mad Dog Madison?
He eats lightning and craps thunder
We wanna eat lightning and crap thunder
Just like Mad Dog Madison!"

The tunnel opened up unexpectedly into an area high enough to sit up straight. He turned around, and in spite of the sharp pain to his side, he pulled his woman to him. She fell into his arms, hugging him tightly, and began to sob quietly.

"It's okay. I'm here," Lucas said gently, stroking her hair. "See down below? There are sunlight streaks, which mean they dug air holes. It's just dark, honey. You can breathe. See?"

"I'm sorr...sorry," she said, her voice muffled against his chest. "Stupid. I was okay until I star...started to pan...nic."

"You're very brave. It's just a mental thing, crawling into a hole."

A minute went by. Her breathing became more normal. "Sorry," she apologized again. "Thanks for making me sing with you. It took my mind off being locked up in pitch darkness."

"Shhhhh."

He massaged her neck and stroked her back. It felt good to finally be holding her this close again. His body was very happy right now, enjoying her soft weight against his, absorbing the female heat. In spite of the sun, he'd been cold all day.

Maybe a few minutes of rest would give his tired body a reprieve. It was all mental. He just needed to convince himself he was fine and could run another ten miles, drag a boulder, make love to a hot woman for hours— He leaned back against the cool rock wall.

"Lucas?"

"Hmm."

"Your hand is up my skirt."

"I know."

"You're a sick man."

"That's the only reason why I'm not kissing you," he told her.

"I didn't mean that kind of sick," she said. "I'm not scared any more."

He didn't stop caressing her. "Do you want me to stop?"

"In a minute or so. But not yet," she murmured. "A little higher. Right. There."

He chuckled softly. His Cupcake must be feeling better. "My hand is dirty from all the stuff we've been doing. Geezus, baby, your panties are wet through already."

Somebody was playing a joke on him. He finally had her where he wanted and he was not in any condition to touch her. He made a little growl of frustration and she giggled.

"Bad timing," she whispered.

"Yeah." He touched the soft flesh between her thigh and panty line. "I want to get in there so...badly."

She moaned softly as he ran a fingernail across the wet material. Damn. It was irresistible. He explored and when she stiffened, he knew he connected with the right spot. He started to rub a little harder.

"Lucas..." she said, her body pushing against his hand. "What are you doing?"

"I don't know," he replied, amused. "What do you think I'm doing?"

Feeling lightheaded, he closed his eyes but his fingers determinedly continued pleasuring her through the flimsy material. He didn't care how he felt, he just wanted to hear her moan. Like that. Softly, in his ear. It turned him on, like sexy music. He would gladly die just to make her come in his arms.

She was grinding hard against his hand now and he obligingly stroked her harder. Her hand flirted with the front of his pants but there was no way she was going to get in there, not in this position. Instead she covered the bulge that was trying desperately to push a hole through his clothes and squeezed lightly. He grunted but didn't relent from his ministration. Her panties were totally wet now, soaking his hand. He slid his other hand down into the back of her panties and cupped that delicious ass, so silky smooth and round. He snuck one finger a little lower, allowing him a tiny, flitting touch. That was just enough to push her over. She shook in his arms as she came.

"You're crazy and I love you," she said into his ear.

He smiled lazily. *Now* he got the lady where he wanted. In love with him. Next step was to get her to marry him. If he survived whatever was eating up his system.

He pushed it out of his mind. Couldn't do anything about that right now. "You're crazier. You attacked a grenade launcher," he reminded her.

"I think I want to attack this one now," she said.

That naughty woman's hand somehow slipped inside his pants over his very aroused, very unprotected warhead. At least one major part of him didn't think he was that sick. He laughed at himself silently.

"Lucas, you're not wearing underwear!"

"I'm not a fucking Airborne Ranger. SEALs don't need no fucking underwear," he told her, lifting her by the waist.

He could run ten miles. He could carry a big boulder. He could make love for hours to a hot woman. Only one way to find out if he was up to the task. Yup. Standing and ready, sir!

CHAPTER THIRTEEN

Shahrukh didn't interrupt the woman pacing back and forth in front of him. Zerya wasn't yet calm enough for a discussion. She swerved around to face him suddenly, her eyes glittering with emotion, her lips pursed in anger.

"You ask too much," she said. "Do you know what you're asking?"

"Am I talking to one of the top officers of the *Peshmerga* warriors?" Shahrukh countered. "Or am I talking to Zerya?"

Her chin went up. "Are you challenging my position? I asked a favor, yes, but it wasn't official. Obviously you're trying to wiggle out of it by changing our agreement. I gave you the names you wanted and you said you'd take care of the traitor."

He shook his head. "No, I said I'd find a name to do your task but he comes with his own price." He lowered his voice. "Perhaps you were being more Zerya at that moment because we were negotiating in bed."

He had no illusions about that part of their relationship at all. Zerya was a Peshmerga warrior first, in or out of bed, but they had also been lovers a long time ago, before she gave her life for a cause, before words and actions became mere items of negotiations.

Her expression softened for an instant before resuming the tough mask. "Rukh, you made it sound like he was going to cost me money. Not going into another battle for him or giving up our stockpile of weapons!"

"You know I deal with, as you call them, treasure hunters. They like...assets," he said. "Some of your weapons, that's all, and a group of men for me to take with me for a small mission. Once that's done, my man will take care of your problem."

Or he would, if Jed didn't agree. It didn't matter now.

"It'll expose us, Rukh. "I was ordered here for a reason."

"I understand. I'll protect our identity. Yes, you lose the weapons, but in exchange, you'll be rid of a pest and can go back to France where you'll be free to do battle. You aren't the type to hide and covertly move things around, Zerya. You'll wither and die."

He spoke the truth. Zerya couldn't last in this country, where everywhere she went, she'd had to hide her true self, playing a submissive role to those she was in command of, just because she was a woman. She had always been a woman of action and a willful one at that. A mountain lioness could not be a lamb for long.

"This young girl you want to use my weapons for...are you in love with her?"

Shahrukh shook his head. "It's a favor." He thought of how brave the child was and how well she took his escape advice. "Yet, she is a young girl whose life I'd like to spare. I have to get to her quickly before she's out of reach, and this is the fastest way to get them to talk to me. Look at it this way, a life for a life, and perhaps a future warrior woman is saved."

Zerya stared down at the papers on a nearby desk, an obstinate expression on her face. He could tell she was trying to find another way. Those weapons, left by insurgents who had run off during the border skirmishes, had been a boon. Transporting them into the hands of other Peshmerga agents outside the country, however, had been one of her major obstacles and having to do so in small numbers at a time had really affected her mission. Shahrukh was offering her another way, but the price was half her stockpile. This was his way of getting what T had referred to as the "government connection" in this whole damn affair. A whole shitload of weapons would do, all right.

He'd done many such negotiations when he was a Temple operative. Such missions were called H-A-X, Hostage/Arms Exchange. Like a game of chess, every one of his moves must be calculated. Sacrifice was sometimes necessary.

"An innocent life is irreplaceable, Zerya," he continued to persuade softly. "That cache of weaponry is cheap in comparison."

And still she hesitated, weighing the pros and cons of his proposal. Shahrukh didn't hurry her, even though time was of the essence, because hers was an equally heavy responsibility too. If exposed, her small army of fighters here would be in even more danger, surrounded by insurgent groups left and right. The Kurds, as a people, had suffered ethnic cleansing and genocide for generations; they had no loyalty left but to their own cause, which was self-survival and statehood. Although his being brought up in the States alienated him from the cultural aspects, these were his people and he understood their fight for recognition and dignity. Those years back with his father and clan had given him both a sense of loss and reunion at the same time, a relationship that pulled at his soul yet simultaneously pushed away his heart.

She finally looked up, revealing the intense storm clashing inside her through her large dark eyes "Those are our people's weapons. I'm going to call Paris and talk it over with them. Give me twenty-four hours."

His heart sank. Twenty four hours. A life time. That little girl's life meant so little to this woman. It was time to use his trump card for the H-A-X. Just as he was about to speak, a series of quick knocks at the door interrupted them.

"Enter," Zerya said in their native dialect.

A man strode in. "Our cameras detected movement, Lieutenant. Two interlopers tripped our wires while moving in the forested area toward our tunnels. Two men with Taliban clothing and they appeared to be looking for something. What do you advise?"

"Can we get to them before they reach the tunnel?" Zerya asked.

"No, we're too far away and someone had removed the shrub covering from it without our noticing it."

"What?" Zerya angrily walked past Shahrukh, snatching the printed photo from the man's hand. "How can that be?"

"The battery in the main camera must have gotten wet. It rained hard last week."

"You expect to use that excuse when the council asks you?"

"No, Lieutenant. I'll take full responsibility."

She slapped the papers back into his hand. "That's good but now we have a big problem. If they find our tunnel, they can call their people and we'll be exposed." She bit her lower lip, then added, "There is no choice. We'll have to head down there and destroy our cache. If we can't have it, no one can."

That he couldn't allow to happen. He wasn't going to let a young life be destroyed because of ego. Once upon a time he might have hesitated about using ruthlessness to fight ruthlessness, but that was before a few years with his unit. He was now a COS Commando, trained to infiltrate and kill from within.

Time to use his trump card. "Zerya," Shahrukh cut in. When she turned to him, he said, "As my father's heir and as head of the clan, I'm ordering you to relinquish your command of your weapons. This is a clan order."

Then he invoked the order using the royal incantation passed to him by his father. The silence in the room thickened with tension as the other two occupants stared at him.

"You'll do as I say in this matter, Lieutenant Zerya."

"You dare—"

"It's done," he told her gently. He turned to the man who immediately saluted him and then giving him the clan show of respect to their elders; he bent slight from the waist, a clench fist against his chest. "Get the necessary contingent ready. And do not blow up the weapons without my say so."

"Yes, Excellency."

* * *

Kit shone her flash light around the cavern they had entered. Now that they were no longer in a confined space, she felt much better. The little shaft of sunlight from the air holes here and there gave the darkness a strange shadowy glow.

"There's a maze of them in here. Are they really all manmade?" She took out her small camera and took a few pictures. She might be able to use this in the article. "You're lucky I have yarn in my backpack. We'd be totally lost in here, with no way out!"

"Too bad that backpack doesn't have a pair of ruby red shoes, Dorothy," Lucas said, shining his downward and ahead. "Watch out here. Don't trip."

She stuck a tongue out at the broad back in front of her. He had to bend his head so as not to hit the jagged cave roof. Other than pausing to look around, though, he appeared to be all right. "How do you walk so surefooted, anyway?"

"What, Ranger brother didn't teach you to walk in the dark? Awww."

"You sound so much better," she mused. His voice was still strangely hoarse, though, and he wasn't walking very fast. Maybe the coolness in the cave was helping. "Almost back to your old self."

"Maybe you have the magic touch, Cupcake." He sounded amused. "Sexual magic."

"I bet all cavemen used that line," she said, mockingly lowering her voice into a Cumber-growl. "Hey, baby, want to cure my sickness? Let's get it on."

He chuckled softly. Then he halted so suddenly, she ran smack into his back. She suddenly found herself flattened against the cave wall behind Lucas' back. He'd moved so quickly she hadn't even managed a squeak of surprise.

"Shh," he said, turning off his flash light and peering around the wall. "If there's anyone there, they'd have heard us but just to be sure...."

"Why do you think there's anyone around?" She whispered.

"I can see piles of stuff all over in the next cave. Nobody there, though."

She squeezed from behind him and peered around the wall too. At first, all she saw were glints reflecting back from different piles. "What do you think they are?"

Lucas clicked his light on again and swept it to the odd-looking mounds. She felt his whole body tense up.

"Weapons," he said. "Hella lotsa weapons."

Her eyes widened at the sight of the number of weaponry. "I thought this place was taken up by our side and searched."

"From what I know, there are networks of tunnels leading to different caverns. They might have missed a few. But damn, this cave holds a hell of a lot they missed."

He cautiously stepped into the cave, waving the flashlight here and there. "Just making sure it's okay to go further, babe. Hang on. Follow me very carefully, okay?"

They made their way to the first grouping.

"Here, shine down on them so I have better lighting," Lucas continued. He went on one knee, held his slim flashlight between his teeth and picked one of the weapons up. He examined it for a minute. Then he looked at another. And another. "Shit."

"What?" She asked, looking over his shoulder.

"They're all well-maintained, newly oiled down. The last border skirmish I read about was a few years ago."

"I remember reading that in my research," Kit said. "It was a huge deal with lots of news articles. They found the insurgents' hiding place and all their weapons. Supposedly.

That guide I told you about said he saw quite a bit carted off by the government, so why are there some here? Another group hiding out here?"

"Possibly," Lucas said, his voice grim.

"But the guide said these caves were regularly monitored by the authorities now."

Lucas sighed. "Yeah, well. Let's just say the government here doesn't monitor as closely as we would like." He stood up. "We have to find the tunnel out of this cave and get to one that's connected to the main ones your guide and all the others know about. If we're lucky and Hawk sent out choppers and saw your message, they'd be heading there and looking for us."

"All right. So, how do we look for this tunnel?" She stared around her dubiously. "It looks impossible."

"Let's start by checking out the sunlight shafts. It's got to be close where they can have air. Someone or some ones come by here often enough to maintain these weapons so let's look for any piles of cleaning cloths and bottles, that sort of thing."

"How about a desk?" Kit asked, pointing to a far off corner. "They might need one to use for cleaning. I bet there will be lots of oils and cleaners near there, if not on it."

He tweaked her hair. "Very good, Watson."

She grinned. "Pfft. I'm Holmes, you're Watson," she declared.

She was right. As they got closer, their light revealed a working space, with a shelf to the right, stacked with bottles and pails. She quickly took several photos while Lucas checked everything out.

"I'm hoping there is an entry near here. If they're using tunnels like the one we were in, logically, they would enter from wherever, light this lamp hanging here on the wall so they could see, wait, I feel some kind of breeze...*voilu!*" He pushed aside a crate, revealing a small entry way big enough to crawl through.

Kit crouched down and felt the air coming from the hole. "Shall we crawl through and—"

A crack sounded behind them. She turned and caught a quick glimpse of shadows and reflection of metal from their flashlights before Lucas pushed her out of the way. A single gunshot exploded, its echo reverberating over and over. She laid on the floor in shock for an instant, then rolled away, looking for a place to hide.

Lucas! Where was Lucas? Was he shot?

She pulled out her gun. She heard a familiar grunt to her right and turned her head, searching for his silhouette. The shafts of sunlight looked like little strobes of dust as shadowy figures fought. Somehow Lucas had managed to run to the other end of the small cavern, disarm one of their assailants and was now engaging in hand-to-hand combat with him on the floor. The other man lifted his big weapon and butted the side of Lucas' head with it. She had no time to scream a warning. Without thinking, she aimed and fired. Dropping his firearm, Lucas' attacker yelled in pain, then fell over.

She clapped a hand over her mouth at what she'd done. The man was in the shadows, rolling around in pain. She shivered and stared at her hand holding her weapon. She'd fired one in self-defense before, when she'd surprised a burglar at her apartment in college. At that time, she was being attacked and she'd gone for her firearm after being chased into her bedroom. The burglar had run off at her first shot and was subsequently caught by the neighbors. This was different and it was frightening how she'd just shot a man as a target.

She took a deep breath. Stay calm. It wasn't the time to be hysterical about it. Her father had told her when he'd taught her how to shoot—*"you're in or you're out when you use this. Don't hesitate."* She stood up and charged towards Lucas, who was still wrestling on the floor. He was at the bottom, after falling over from the hit in the head. She kicked away the offending machine gun lying nearby.

"Hoo-yahhh!" She yelled and launched on top of the enemy pounding on her man.

She pulled at the man's hair and punched him in the throat. Scratched. Gouged. He was howling and turning around to grab her fists.

Someone pulled her off from behind. She struggled valiantly but didn't have the strength. The person grabbed her arms and pulled them back. She yelped in pain and twisted back and forth, trying to free herself.

Lucas must have heard her because he let out a roar of anger and somehow stood up, with his attacker still attached on him, and half-leapt-half-stumbled onto her assailant. Then, yet another pair of arms grabbed her. Only then was she aware of many voices surrounding them. How many of them were there? She'd only seen two when Lucas was fighting.

She watched Lucas tackle one man and another jumped in from behind. Punches flew. Lucas threw one body across the room. She screamed his name and struggled as yet another shadowy figure appeared and another, till she couldn't see him under so many bodies.

Someone yelled something out in Arabic. Kit blinked from the sudden light. There were men everywhere, some of whom were holding lanterns. Except for a howling man still rolling on the floor and another being held at gun point, these were in military uniform. To her surprise, a woman appeared, in camouflage shirt and pants. She studied Kit for a second then turned toward the men on the floor.

"Five of you against one man?" She asked, in perfect English. "We must be getting soft."

In the brighter light, Kit could only see Lucas' leg and she anxiously waited as the male bodies on top moved out of the way, leaving one man pointing a weapon straight at Lucas. She whimpered at the sight of blood on his face but dared not move or say anything, in case it'd set him off.

He appeared calm, though. He slowly turned his head.

"Kit." His voice came out in a hoarse growl

"Here. I'm okay," she hastily assured him.

The woman stepped forward. "It's okay, soldier, I'm Lieutenant Zeravich from the 210th Division. I apologize to

163

have mistaken you as the enemies. We're here to transport you." She turned to her men. "Take the two prisoners out of here."

Kit frowned as the men obeyed her orders. Although all of them were in fatigues, Arab head gear covered much of their faces. She was quite sure not all of them were Americans. After putting hoods over the two who had attacked them first, they tossed the injured man she'd shot—she breathed a sigh of relief he was alive—over one man's shoulder and led the other out, using the trail she and Lucas earlier had been on. While that was happening, someone else searched Lucas for weapons, pulling out his pockets and patting down his pants. That didn't seem friendly protocol either.

After a minute of silence, Lucas confirmed her suspicions. "There isn't a fucking 210th Division. Who are you?" he asked, still lying on the ground.

"Again, I apologize," the woman said. "When I saw you were Americans, I needed to give our prisoners the impression we're on the same side. A woman in charge ought to convince them, don't you think?"

Her smile had a glimmer of amusement.

"I repeat, who the hell are you?" Lucas asked.

"Not your business, soldier. Let's just say for now we're the owners of these weapons."

Kit hoped they weren't going to search her too. She didn't want to lose her camera and important things. The man holding her prisoner seemed satisfied with just twisting her arms behind her back, though.

"Lieutenant, I found this card on him. Read the name on it." One of the rough-looking men who had been searching Lucas' pockets held up a scrap of paper.

The woman took it from him. After a moment, she said, "Why am I not surprised?" She turned towards one of the waiting men. "Tell him he can come in."

The underling went off to one side and Kit watched him disappear behind what looked like a protruding piece of rock. How many tunnels were there in this place?

"Except for the bump on his head, he is not injured, Lieutenant," the searcher said.

"Let him sit up. I suggest you obey orders, soldier. No sudden lunges. Remember, we also have your woman friend here as a prisoner." The Lieutenant turned at the sound of someone re-entering the cavern from the rocky protrusion. Kit fancied she heard a thread of anger in her voice as she greeted the man who appeared. "Excellency, I believe this man has your card, so perhaps you know him."

Kit looked up and her eyes widened. Whoever the new guy was, she could tell he was in charge. He was tall, like Lucas, with fierce-looking dark eyes, assessing the situation with one sweeping glance. A machine gun slung carelessly over one shoulder. And was that...yikes...a sword? A big-ass shiny out-of-medieval-times sword with a curved blade. In the muted lighting from the lanterns, he looked imposing and dangerous.

A small smile appeared on his lips when he saw Lucas on the floor. The light caught the gleam of an earring as he swung his gaze toward her. She swallowed, meeting his eyes. Then again wished she had her camera handy. It would so cool to have his photo on her tablet wallpaper.

"I know Lucas Branson here. Who are you?" He asked, his American accent making her blink in surprise.

"Kit," she replied. Did Lucas really know him? "Who are you?"

His smile widened. "An American woman in a Pakistani dress running around in a cave with a weapon. I was watching you on the camera. You should be a GEM operative." He nodded to the man behind her. "Release her."

"A what?" Kit asked.

He didn't answer her. Instead, turning to Lucas, who was still watching him, he said, "Why are you here, Branson, and where is your team? I notice you're not on your feet. May I ask if your wound is bothering you?"

Kit inhaled. Lucas was indeed holding his side again. How badly was that cut he said he had? She frowned. A new worry gnawed at her. Had he been lying and it wasn't food poisoning that was making him sick like that?

* * *

Lucas shook his head. This whole damn day had been like riding on a rollercoaster. He was all for action, but everything usually made sense, especially about which group belonged to which side. And now, here was the same fucking dude from last night. Then he was just some middle-man with connections. Now, he was all dressed up like he was some warlord with his own tribe. What the hell?

He examined him up and down. He looked cleaned-up and certainly better groomed than his own current self. AK-47 over one shoulder. Was that a freaking broad sword? Did people even use that anymore? Rounds of ammo criss-crossed his chest. There were knives sheathed in his belt and the sides of his boots. What, did the dude think he was fucking Rambo?

He was beyond pissed-off at the moment. He couldn't get over how weak he was. Yesterday, he would have handled a dozen of these assholes without hesitation. Right now, he was out of breath and his side was burning a hole into his stomach. He refused to be sick in front of these guys, whoever they were.

"Give me the 411 on what's happening, Shahrukh. I'm not talking until I know who these fu...people are," he demanded.

"I don't think you're in the position to be asking questions, soldier!" the woman who had clued him in on everything being a ruse told him sharply.

"He's a SEAL, Lieutenant Zerya. They prefer to be called sailor," Shahrukh corrected mildly. "Branson, they're my people. You're in the middle of an operation I'm running."

"Weapons? In insurgent-infested caves? Your story stinks."

"Does it matter? All I need is to call Hawk to confirm. But first, you have to tell me why you're here."

Lucas shook his head again. No way was he going to be specific. "Long story, but it has to do with the girl at that wedding thing we...attended. Do you remember?"

Shahrukh cocked his head, a frown forming. "Minah. Yes."

"You know Minah?" Kit asked, leaning forward eagerly. "Do you know how to find her? She is—"

"A friend," Lucas interrupted. "We're trying to get hold of her. But first, we must contact Hawk and Jazz. We need to tell them our location."

"No need," Shahrukh said, pressing a finger in his ear, listening. Lucas realized he must be wearing a wire. "Ah. Choppers very close by. Lieutenant Zeravich, please leave me four men and follow my earlier orders. Lucas, you and Miss...Kit can come with me. It seems they somehow have tracked you down. How?"

"Kit sent them a message," Lucas said. "We found the back way instead of the front entrance and were making our way there when we found your little cache here. What do you intend to do with it? Because I'll be reporting it to my commander."

The snooty woman, Lieutenant Zeravich, made a rude noise and said something in a language Lucas didn't recognize. Shahrukh replied likewise. The woman answered and turned her back on him rudely. Shahrukh just nodded to the men and they started heading toward the different piles on the floor.

Lucas tried to stand up and barely made it without stumbling back on his knee. "You better have a good explanation where you're taking them, Shahrukh," he warned.

Kit came running over. He hoped she wouldn't bring up the fact that he wasn't one hundred percent, although he had a feeling the other man had his suspicions.

"I'm okay," he assured her.

Her eyes narrowed slightly. She turned to Shahrukh. "Excuse me, did you say you know Minah? And that people are here to rescue us?" She glanced at Lucas again. "I really, really need to get hold of Minah. Please."

"I know," Shahrukh said. His voice was gentle. "I'll get to her soon, I hope."

Lucas looked up sharply. "What do you mean?"

"Let's just get your commander's attention first, shall we? There isn't time to lose." He started toward the bigger opening, the one with rock protrusion. "Coming, or not?"

"Yeah," Lucas replied.

What choice did he have? He needed to get to Hawk or Jazz, but he was certain by the time he conveyed to them about the weapons in this particular cavern, they would be gone. He glanced back at the men efficiently picking them up. There was a shitload of them. If he hurried, maybe his team could stop them. He took a step. And another. Fucking hell. His legs felt like he had 100lb weights tied to his ankles.

He looked down at Kit. Those pretty blue eyes showed so much worry, he wanted to kiss her and tell her he was okay. Instead, he just smiled and gave her a thumbs up. "No cadences, please," he teased, hoping his smile didn't look like a grimace as pain gnawed one side of him.

He was a SEAL. He wasn't going to show he was in trouble. Dig in. Walk straight. Deep breath. Power on. He'd noticed if he shouted and let adrenalin take over, the nausea and pain would become worse. If he kept his head straight, he should be A-OK until he was back at base.

"So I'm gathering the yarn was your idea of not getting lost?"

"Yes. But I was getting worried, with so many tunnels, whether I'd have enough!"

"Then I arrived just in time."

"Yeah! Those two other men...I shot one of them because he hit Lucas in the head. What's your name again? And what exactly do you do?"

"You're a good shot. I'm just a friend of Lucas and his team, that's all."

"You must give an interview to me and *my* team."

"And what exactly do you do, Kit?"

Kit and Shahrukh seemed to be getting along like a house on fire. Lucas didn't like it at all. Not one bit.

As they continued, he could hear the thump-thump-thump outside. Ahead, a small crack of light. He concentrated on it, watching it getting bigger and bigger as he struggled to walk without stumbling. His commander, Hawk McMillan, was already off the chopper heading towards the mouth of the cave when they slipped out of the cool darkness. Lucas looked around. Thank God. Familiar faces.

Lucas snapped a salute. Hawk returned one and put a hand up to halt the situation report he'd formed.

"One moment, Cumber," he said, then turned to Shahrukh. "You're damn quick. T contacted me while I was in the air regarding your situation and your current operation. Tell me you didn't know about these weapons beforehand before I give you my help."

Lucas blinked. Damn, he didn't even have to tell anything and those COS commandos and GEM operatives had already taken over.

"I didn't know about these weapons," Shahrukh said.

Hawk's gaze was laser-direct and a bit skeptical. "You have thirty minutes, tops, before the authorities of either side of these borders reach here."

"We have enough to convince you and your counterparts to buy me time to set things up." Shahrukh gazed up the mountain trail. "You have to release the weapons to me for now."

"His men are already removing them, Sir!" Lucas volunteered the information.

"Shahrukh, it's against protocol to move weapons around and then recollect them at another checkpoint," Hawk said. "Those weapons are important to show how much the insurgents around here are preparing for battle."

"I'm sure Mrs. Zeringue and Miss Hutchens would disagree about the amount of importance weighed against a girl's life," Shahrukh said calmly. "It is a girl's life we're trying to save, is it not? And in the end, you'll get your weapons, with a little fire power, to show the other side you mean business. If we succeed, then you'll have weapons and a recorded battle to show for it. What good is a find if you're without a group to which to point a finger in your many reports?"

Lucas noted Shahrukh's demeanor never changed through his argument. He sounded like a logic professor, giving the details to reach a projected conclusion. The dude was a great strategist but how good was he in a real war, with many variations to a scenario? He was sure his commander was considering all the possibilities of things going wrong now as he too glanced up the mountainside.

"And what are we going to do for distraction?" He asked.

"You'll need to move your copters toward the target. I'll call and let you know where and when. I have the advantage of being on horseback and getting to the area to...set things up. We also have two men, one injured. You may want to keep them for questioning, although they'll tell you they didn't have any knowledge of the weapons. But they're local Taliban fighters and it'd be a good idea to keep them behind bars for a while. Your people here," Shahrukh continued, pointing at Lucas and Kit, with a quick smile at her, "surprised them. Kit shot at one of them."

Hawk turned to Kit. "My co-commander talked to your media crew. Sean Cortez is burning a hole through the floor back on base. I'm not sure whether it's out of worry for you or because I forbade him to come along on our Chinook." His flash of amusement suggested the latter. He added, "Jazz found your van. When he searched around it, he found newspaper articles about a certain bin Yakob. We have quite a number of questions for Mr. Cortez."

Lucas caught his commander's gaze and gave him a shrug, indicating he had no idea. But this Cortez fellow must trying to sniff out details other than the plight of Pashtun women. He remembered Kit saying something about Minah's description of a raid during her interview. If Cortez listened to that recording and investigate further, he'd realize the Cob had recently been secretly captured by the US army. He needed to let Hawk know about the interview back at the school.

"Oh, Sean! I totally forgot about him and the others." Kit turned to Lucas. "You can go back and let him know I'm okay, right? You can take my backpack and the suitcase to him. Tell him the passports and important stuff are in there."

Lucas frowned. "What are you talking about? You're coming with me. You can give them to him yourself. I've never met the guy."

Kit gave him an impatient wave and approached Shahrukh. "Mr. Shahrukh, sir, can I ride horseback with you to wherever it is you're planning to get Minah? I'm so worried about her and besides, the firsthand information will really help the news piece I told you about. We could conduct the interview afterwards too."

She spoke so earnestly, no one could deny that sweet plea in her voice.

Oh no. Oh hell, no to the nth. Not. Nein. No way.

Lucas took a swift step forward, swept a surprised Kit over one shoulder, glared at Shahrukh, and practically ran toward the chopper. He ignored Kit's "Hey!" and quick protests. Oh no. She wasn't going to go anywhere with that commando without him around. He could see she was all smitten with that stupid broad sword and Rambo attitude.

He reached the Chinook and Mink was there. Depositing her in his friend's arms, he climbed up quickly, pulled her back into his arms, then turned sideways and gagged for a full minute.

"You look like shit," Mink remarked.

"Long day, dude," Lucas managed in between gasps of air and coughing.

He kept a firm hold on a very mad Cupcake, then grinned. In his hurry, he'd forgotten to ask permission from his commander to leave. The woman was all sorts of trouble.

He returned her to Mink.

"Don't let her go. That's an order," he said, then jumped off the copter again, gathering all his reserves to make it back to Hawk to stand in attention. His commander and Shahrukh were looking at him like he was an idiot.

"Pardon me, sir! That woman is under the illusion she's an Airborne Ranger, sir!"

"An Airborne Ranger?" Hawk asked, amused, looking back at the Chinook. "She's cussing you out like she's one, Cumber."

"I'd admit she's been tough. She single-handedly stopped a grenade exploding by accelerating the speed of our vehicle. Said she heard about it from her brother, an Airborne Ranger."

"Is that what happened? Jazz sent me a picture of that baby stuck in the grill. Damn lucky. Or maybe not, if Miss Kit had planned it."

"She's amazing," Lucas told him proudly, then straightened again, adding firmly, "But she isn't going anywhere with Shahrukh."

"I was going to say no," Shahrukh said, humor in his voice. "But when you lauded her warrior abilities like that, I might need her quick thinking and reckless bravery. After all, I did see her coming to your rescue back there, against those two insurgents."

"Two insurgents," Hawk repeated. His gaze turned sharp. "Branson, you shouldn't have any trouble with two hostiles. What's the matter?"

Lucas stared straight ahead. He wasn't going to admit any weaknesses in front of the other man. "Nothing, sir. I was fighting in the dark and got slammed in the head with a weapon. Kit just joined in. She needn't have. She's under my charge and I'm determined to return her in one piece back to her friends."

Hawk studied him for a second. "You're full of it, Cumber," he said, softly. "I'll take her back myself. At ease. Let go. I'll take care of her, I promise."

Lucas finally met his commander's eyes. He'd have argued if he could, but the ground was rocking under his feet as if there was an earthquake in the area. He just wanted to make sure Kit was going to be safe. Hawk would make sure of that.

"Thank you, sir," he said. He let out a sigh.

Without another word, he pitched forward, watching detachedly as the ground rose up to meet him. Damn, there was something else. But it was too late. Everything went black.

* * *

Kit couldn't believe it. Did he just caveman her? She glared after his broad back as he walked to his commander and Shahrukh. She twisted and turned but Mink refused to loosen his hold. She called him a few choice names.

"Sorry, Kit. I'm on orders to keep you with me," he told her, flashing his trademark grin at her.

"Lucas! I'm so going to...dammit, let me go! Mink, I'm going to hurt you so...Lucas!" Kit let out a small gasp when she saw Lucas falling forward and both his commander and Mr. Shahrukh hurrying forward to catch him. "Lucas! Mink, you have to let me go. Lucas needs help!"

"Damn. What's going on?" Mink put her down on her feet. "Come on."

They both ran toward the group, followed closely by Dirk. When she got to him, Lucas was out cold. Mr. Shahrukh was checking his pulse.

"Lucas!" She knelt down beside him. "He told me he had food poisoning. He's been coughing and vomiting the last few hours. He passed out once already."

"Food poisoning?" Hawk asked.

She nodded. "Some bad breakfast, he said. I kept giving him water to stay hydrated but I could tell he wasn't feeling well. He panted a lot and was too quiet when we were hiking through the brush. I knew something was wrong because he even let me lead the way a time or two, until he realized it, then he would take the lead again."

"Couldn't be breakfast," Mink said. "Dirk and I ate the same stuff and we're fine."

"Fine! I hate that word! That's what he would say every time I asked him. 'I'm fine, don't worry,' 'It's just some bad food, I'm fine, Cupcake,'" she mimicked Lucas' deep voice in disgust. "I knew he was lying. Knew it."

"He just wanted to get you to safety," Hawk said. He glanced at Mr. Shahrukh. "What you said last night about his wound. He went through tests but the results didn't show anything."

"Herbal poisoning is hard to detect," Shahrukh murmured, kneeling down beside Kit.

Wound? Poison? Kit grabbed Shahrukh's sleeve. "What are you talking about? He told me he had a little cut." She frowned, remembering. "He kept grabbing his side. And it was bleeding again for a while but he assured me it was because the stitches broke."

She started pulling up Lucas' shirt. Shahrukh helped her, parting the material. The sight of the "cut" made her gag.

There was an open wound, like sliced raw meat, at the side of Lucas' body, just on the inside of his hips. A huge bruise surrounded the crater, which was oozing blackish looking liquid. There were nasty white blisters forming like little islands inside the bloody mess. It didn't look like a regular wound at all.

"Fuck," Mink said quietly. "It was just a mere puncture wound when I sewed it. Let me get the first-aid kit."

As he ran back to the helicopter, Kit pulled off her backpack and rummaged through it. She found what she was looking for—rubbing alcohol and some wads of cotton. Shahrukh took the bottle from her and undoing the cap, he poured it liberally on the wound.

"The poison worked its way into his system, first infesting the wound and then infecting his blood," he said, carefully examining the open wound, his fingers prodding the flesh here and there. "That's why he was vomiting. Without the blade that cut him, I won't know what poisoned him."

Mink came back with a box. Dirk was with him and gave Kit a grin of acknowledgment. He leaned over to look and shook his head in disbelief.

"I saw him with it this morning," he said. "Check his side pockets. He might have stuck it in one of them,"

"Iodine?" Mink asked, pulling out medication and a needle. "Would an anti-fungal shot help?"

"Mr. Shahrukh's men patted him down and took all his weapons," Kit said. "I don't remember a blade."

"Try his ankles," Mink suggested. "Cumber would have made sure to have a hidden weapon."

Hawk, who was kneeling at the far end of Lucas, rolled up the pant leg. A handle of a small knife in a soft leather holster stuck out from the top of his sock. Pulling it out, he handed it to Shahrukh.

"It wasn't all embedded in him or anything," Dirk supplied the information. "It went through his belt. That's why he wasn't too worried."

Shahrukh examined the knife and sniffed at where the handle and blade met. He nodded. "I can smell it. Sweet clover and castor oil. Give him that anti-fungal injection, it can't hurt, but you'll need my antidote. I have a salve but that's just external. In his condition, you'll need to wake him up and feed him the antidote every hour for the next six. I can't be there with him, so I'm leaving that one of your responsibilities." He gave them all a swift encompassing glance. "If you leave him in the care of the medics on base while all of you go off on mission, there is no guarantee they'll follow my instructions because it's not hospital medication."

"We don't have time to go back to base," Hawk said. "Our plan was to meet you up there with the help of our river crew. No Chinook. They'll just shoot us down. We'll strike when you give the signal."

"But what about Lucas?" Kit asked. She was beginning to feel afraid for him.

"We'll have to take a chance and leave him in the Chinook if he doesn't wake up."

"I hope you're aware that castor oil is one of the ingredients in ricin," Shahrukh said, "He needs my antidote hourly or he'll go into kidney failure. And he needs to be awake to drink it."

Kit could feel her anger reaching boiling point. The big lug. The macho idiot. She took out her camera and snapped photos of the horrible looking wound.

"What's that for?" Mink asked.

"Hey, he's got to see this so he won't ever lie to me again when I ask him whether he's all right. I'll just whip this pic out and show him the last time he thought he was fine!" Kit told him. Also, it would be part of her news item about warriors in the Pakistan-Afghanistan border. She glared down at Lucas, put her face right next to his and busted out her Sergeant voice. Hands on hip, she yelled out, "Cu-Cum-Ber! You lazy sod of a Navy SEAL, if you don't get up and take these meds like a man, I'll start singing Airborne Ranger cadences at your funeral and make you squirm in that fucking casket. Come on! Get. Up! *I wanna be an Airborne Ranger!*"

She didn't pay attention to the stunned men around her as she coaxed her guy to wake up. If he didn't, he was going to die.

What was that song he'd been singing to her? "*We wanna be tough like Mad Dog Madison! How tough is Mad Dog Madison?* Come on, Cucumber! How tough is Mad Dog Madison?"

A groan escaped Lucas' lips. His eyes still shut, he slowly turned and started to get on his knees.

"He eats lightning and craps thunder," he mumbled.

"I. Can't. Hear. You!" Kit shouted. "What do we want to do?"

Lucas stood up straight and stood at attention. His eyes were half-opened. "We wanna eat lightning and crap thunder!" His voice came out in a growl. Then his eyes snapped wide open and he sang, "Just like Mad Dog Madison!"

Another moment of stunned silence.

"Hawk, sir, we have to hire her," Dirk said in admiration. "She can wake and command an army of Zombie Cumbers."

CHAPTER FOURTEEN

Shahrukh nudged his horse forward. The last glow of daylight played an eerie dusty trail across the sky. It was a photogenic shot, the kind one would see in a magazine, with the majestic backdrop of craggy mountains and lush green valleys. A world the people here claimed as the real location of the Garden of Eden.

He enjoyed the magnificent sight for a moment. It wouldn't be long before such peace was shattered by another world, one created by humans, as they'd done for thousands of years over this piece of land. A world where the ancient warfare of horse and swords met with the high-tech wizardry of machine gun and satellite communications.

The tribal wars here were mostly ignored by the authorities from both sides. The prevailing wisdom was a "let them kill each other" attitude. It was also a strange combination of clan loyalty since both Afghanistan and Pakistan had Pashtun and other ethnic heritage and they understood the long history of the tribal traditions.

Pashtunwali, the code of honor by which all Pashtuns lived. Shahrukh turned his animal around and waited for his men bringing the prisoner. Well, prisoner was too strong a word. Perhaps, temporary guest, since he was given no choice for this meeting.

"I'm honored to have a chance to talk to one of the elder of the *jirga*," he told the older man in perfect Pashto. His kind had mingled in these parts long enough to be assimilated into the culture. "I apologize in the manner you were brought here but this is an urgent matter that will affect the lives of those in your clan and I have no wish to start a war with yours."

The man had his poker face on, merely lifting his white brows slightly. "I'm not a guest. I'm here without being asked. How is that a good start to anything?"

Shahrukh bowed his head slightly. Being a guest in *pashtunwali* had many meanings. "My apologies again. I don't have time on my side. Your clan has an ongoing *badal* with Yakob's people. He has had a few of your own family murdered. You have also done likewise to some of his clan. Yet, you've ordered a young girl from your side named Minah to be given to Yakob, as *swara*, to end the *badal*. I know she ran away and one of your relatives caught and returned her to Yakob's side. Yakob isn't with them any more. As you are aware, he has been kidnapped by the Americans."

"So many kidnappings. What is it to you?"

"His clan isn't happy about this and suspects a betrayal on your side about his presence at the ceremonial home the other night. They plan to continue the *badal*, even though they now have Minah." Shahrukh pointed in the direction of the other man's tribal stronghold. "Even as I speak, they are planning to burn down some of your homes."

The other many visibly stiffened. "I see. And why are you telling me this?"

"Yakob has used me and my good will. After procuring weapons from me, he betrayed me. I intend to exact my own revenge for the dishonor he's caused. I need you to facilitate the delivery of these weapons as part of your exchange to end the *badal* between your people and his clan. Once my men have entered, you may leave and not look back. Your *badal* ends there. As a further show of my gratitude of your helping me restore my honor, I'll pay for the restoration of your burnt homes and will send a year's worth of food for your immediate family."

The last bit was important. Food was a much needed item in many of the mountain villages.

If the old elder agreed, once his side had delivered the weapons, the US troops would have a reason to attack that stronghold. It would be his chance to enter into the fray and find Minah. He already knew where she was probably kept. A *swara* marriage, the bride given away as a replacement, meant she was no higher than a yard animal. Her new family would not be treating her well. The poor girl would be kept in the barn, just as her marriage had been conducted outside one. In *pashtunwali*, one member must bear all the honor and the other must bear all the shame. It didn't matter if the latter was an innocent party.

The elder looked up thoughtfully into the sky. "I agree," he finally said. "If you see my granddaughter, kill her. If she runs back home, she would start another round of violence. I have told her this but she's obstinate, that one."

Shahrukh thought of the young girl who had so bravely trusted his advice that night not so long ago. The desperation in her eyes had made his heart hurt. She was too young to understand her ties with her family were gone, yet already old enough to know if she didn't take a chance then, she'd be forever shackled as an animal.

"Consider her dead," he grimly told the elder.

* * *

Lucas swallowed down the vile potion Kit handed him. He didn't need to say a word. Her eyes told him if he didn't do exactly that, she would think of a way to make him comply. Besides, his team was on her side. Somehow, within the short span of meeting them, she'd gained their admiration.

"Don't look so smug," he told her. "They're just in awe of the goodies in your backpack."

It was true. Inside the Chinook, they'd gathered around while she pulled out some of her loot. Camera, guns, knives, spray paint, small medical kit, mini tablet laptop, utensils, shoelaces, yarn, notebook, mini recorder, chocolate, energy bars, deodorant, socks...the list went on. Lucas had explained how she'd used the yarn and Mink had told him they'd seen her spray paint on the scarf waving like a flag over the top of the tree. She had also added a large frog, with four legs spread out, so there was no mistaking it was a message to "froggers." That was what finally persuaded them to take the risk and go to the nearest caves.

"Damn clever, Kit," Mink said, with a smile.

"Isn't she?" Lucas said, proudly.

They met the rest of the team waiting with the gunboat crew. From the quick briefing given by Hawk, he understood there was no time to waste. They needed to speed off to the best possible vantage point, where Amber had mapped out from this morning, for this second mission. It was now obvious to those who had questioned about her being on their boat now recognized her importance. Through her CIA channels, she'd pinpointed which tribal lookout point belonged to the Taliban and which one would look the other way if necessary because of age old enmity and power struggles. Tonight, they needed one of those lookout points because of the large collection of men and weapons being confiscated from Point B to Point A.

Everyone was ready. He could feel the bite of anticipation in the air as last minute orders were taken care of and satellite calls came and went, updating Hawk and all the men on what was happening in the mountains as well as at the US Central Command, where Admiral Madison was getting all the generals and the upper echelons of the political stage on one page.

He hadn't really trusted the undercover operative, Shahrukh, much when they'd first met, but the man sure knew how to get things done quickly. The immense responsibility he was currently carrying was sobering. He had to satisfy all political fronts, enabling a US deployment of power by timing a weapons delivery so they could be captured. The cache would in turn placate the ruling Afghan and Pakistan parties, especially since they were from a Taliban controlled area.

Also, Shahrukh had to prevent any misunderstood flare-up between yet another local warlord and the US presence. Lucas wasn't sure how he managed to get someone to deliver the weapons without arousing suspicions, but from listening to his co-commanders communicate with him and each other, he'd achieved that objective. Lastly, and perhaps the most important of all, he was in charge of bringing back the missing girl. If things did come in threes, Lucas wished the man every success in that last endeavor. The latter was putting his life at risk, personally going in to make a rescue of someone he didn't even know.

Knowing from experience how dangerous such an act was, Lucas' respect for the commando had grown exponentially. Also, he owed him his kidney, if not his life. He hadn't had a chance to properly thank him.

Right now he felt like he'd had gone a few rounds with a champion boxer. He'd already caught hell from both his commanders and his woman. He supposed he should have shown more concern about that cut, especially when Shahrukh had warned him, but it was such a small nick. How was he supposed to know it would get all infected like some kind of alien bug had crawled into his body? He'd examined it and secretly admitted it looked horrific. The salve Shahrukh had placed on it had helped ease the fiery burn and he seemed to be able to think clearer. Maybe that unpleasant potion he was forcing down his throat was really some kind of antidote.

While the others went off to take their positions, he'd been given the lighter duty of sniper post, where he didn't have to move out of position.

He gave Kit a stern look. "You stay in that hatch. You don't come out. You don't take pictures. Or I'll tie your hands up and you can spank me later."

Her eyes narrowed. Then she grinned. "You promise?"

He gave her a reluctant grin but resisted flirting back. His friends were watching and the Stooges were elbowing each other.

"Kit, don't put others' lives at stake because of a few pictures," he said instead.

She rolled her eyes. "Of course not. I'll do as I'm told. My brother is—"

"A fucking Airborne Ranger!" roared the Stooges and a few others.

Obviously, they'd all been filled in with the details. They chuckled as Kit gave them the finger. A minute later, his commander gave the signal and they started upriver, the huge boat slithering like a shadowy monster under the darkening skies.

When they stopped, Lucas glanced at Kit. She nodded and after handing him yet another vial of antidote, she quietly climbed into her hatch.

"And now, we wait," Hawk mouthed.

* * *

Shahrukh climbed off his steed. He'd already given the signal to Jazz Zeringue. His men inside had their orders. The first explosion and they were to fan out in different directions. Their job was to compromise the exits, then allow the SEALs and the other military outfits with them to do their jobs.

The Kurdish blood in him demanded he join in but he had another assignment. His men were war-conditioned, experienced in the art of stealthy attacks. They would take advantage of these insurgents and disappear into the night.

He already had messages passed around through the hotbed of insurgent tribes. Whispered through the channels, the news would spread about this particular mistake by the clan.

Who would be so stupid as to take in weapons when they had just been attacked the previous night?

Didn't they know they were being watched? Surely we could not trust them to be in our network.

They're Taliban. Of course the US would watch them and attack. We must not join forces with them.

Shahrukh had no problem with the border wars. That was for the people to decide. But the Taliban, with their subjugation of unwilling people and their association with Al-Qaeda, was a different animal altogether. Fewer insurgent groups joining them would be a good setback for a while.

The first explosion hit the front wall.

It had begun.

* * *

Kit heard the distant boom and knew the attack had started. She'd never felt so tense in her life. She wasn't afraid—not really—but her heart was beating hard and her senses appeared to have fingers, reaching out for and grasping every sound, smell and taste, until they echoed like rolling thunder in her brain.

The hatch had some kind of battery-operated lighting and she could peer out through the slight crack of the small entry way. Nothing to see, really. But the noise fed her imagination.

* * *

Shahrukh remembered how the first group of SEALs snuck inside during the initial attack and seizure, through the hole under the barn. He wondered whether Yakob's people found it. It might not have occurred to them, since the invasion happened so quickly. He recalled a hole through the ceiling that had been shot out by somebody. There was a chance they'd thought the attackers had broken inside that way.

He circled the wall in the dark, heading toward where the barn was situated. That Branson fellow was a big man and if he could fit through that hole, Shahrukh would too.

A small grenade exploded behind the wall and a body fell to the ground nearby. He kept on going. His men would open up the side entrance soon and there would be plenty of mayhem.

* * *

"Cumber, position, over." His commander's voice came over his helmet mic.

"Position 3, over. I have my eyes trained for the Shah," Lucas replied quietly. They'd given Shahrukh that moniker. "I'll cover him if he's successful."

He tried to stay positive. He didn't doubt his team and the few gunboat crew members would win and retain the weaponry Shahrukh had used as bait, but he had his doubts about the latter's finding a young girl in the melee. Sure, he'd recognize her and she might even attempt to escape again, but this time, the risks were higher. If she were running around in that big area where the men were engaging in deadly combat, chances are she'd get caught in the middle of some heavy artillery fire.

Shahrukh had told them the women would probably be in hiding in the main house, although the Taliban did sometimes have a nasty habit of using their women as shields or even as weapons. But that was mainly when they planned some kind of attack, such as strapping explosives on a woman to act as a human bomb in the market place.

Still, Lucas hoped Kit was mentally prepared she might not see the young girl alive again. She'd spent the whole day totally invested in her safety and well-being. Losing her when she thought all might end well would be devastating.

The explosions were getting more numerous. His comrades had already taken off, running towards the entrances illuminated by the fires inside. His eyes scanned the terrain, looking for signs of hostiles and Shahrukh.

* * *

Shahrukh went down on his hands and knees. That hole was still there and it was damn small. Those three SEALs must have crawled on their stomachs, which accounted for all that foul animal offal stuck on their uniforms that night. He remembered the smell all too well. He would have to leave most of his weapons and hang on to his main one while crawling in.

He stood up to unstrap his belt and rounds of ammunition. The sound of heavy breathing caught his attention. A small hand reached out from the hole and grabbed his shoe. A shriek followed and the hand receded. Without losing a beat, he was back on his knees, reaching in with his long arm and finding a limb. Determinedly fighting biting teeth and sharp nails, he tugged hard and pulled a screaming, struggling body out of the hole.

He covered her mouth. The skin felt slippery from all the muck she'd crawled through.

"It's me," he said in Pashto, shaking her. "Ahmin."

That was his Pashtun name when he mingled among the clans.

She was sobbing, almost hysterical. "Ahmin, Ahmin, Ahmin," she chanted.

"Do you remember me?"

"Yes, yes, yes. Help me. They caught me again. Help me." She threw herself on him, her voice filled with a desperation that would haunt him later.

"I'm here to help you," he told her. "Be that brave girl again for me. Stop crying. We have to go but you must stop acting like a child and be brave now."

She was crying so hard, her tears soaked through the front of his shirt. His hands were wet. Her neck felt slippery. Her hair was a mass of wet tangles and goop stuck to it. Her breathing sounded very raspy, as if she was having difficulty breathing through her sobs. He frowned. Something wasn't right.

"I will stop crying. I will stop crying." She kept repeating the line.

But her breathing remained horrible, sounding like she was suffering from asthma. Shahrukh quickly restrapped his weapons and then tugged on her arm toward the shrubs and line of trees leading to the hidden pathways. She stumbled behind him. He recalled she'd been more nimble last night. Had she been beaten? Was she injured?

He paused and turned her face toward the illuminated destruction behind them. A curse escaped his lips. He had difficulty checking the tide of anger engulfing him as he stared down at the young face.

They had cut off Minah's nose.

* * *

Lucas aimed. Fired. No outside help. That was Shahrukh's suggestion to Hawk. He'd told them his sources would spread the word it was a tribal warfare. Many would stay away if there was a blood feud, but there would be some who might be clan related coming in to assist.

Joker was on the opposite side doing the same thing. The walled area, which housed the main living areas and the storage facilities, was bursting out in flames all over. There were shouts and war cries, sounds from fleeing panicked horses and people running out. The firelight made it easy to see the men trying to escape.

A lone figure on horseback charged up the dark trail. Lucas aimed his weapon at him. He seemed to know his way, heading toward the meeting place, not far from where the rest of the river crew waited.

It was Shahrukh.

And he was being followed by three other men on horses. One fired his weapon. Shahrukh's horse continued its way through the night towards where Lucas was in position. The three men continued the chase.

Lucas took careful aim and fired.

* * *

When his steed entered the clearing through the shrubbery, Shahrukh let out a whistle, then nudged his horse back into the shadows. Minah was hunched over in front of him, her hands grabbing to the mane for dear life. He patted her back gently, then jumped off his horse.

"Minah, you can let go now," he told her in a gentle voice. "It's safe to let go. Jump down."

She'd been very quiet since his outburst, as if his fury calmed her. She unclenched her fists and slid into his arms. He carried her like the child she still was—should be—and not some married woman to a warlord three times her age.

A whistle came back. Then another from the river.

All clear.

He started toward the boat. Same procedure as last night. He regretted he hadn't been able to snatch the young girl somehow then. She wouldn't have had to go through her ordeal then.

The same crew met with him and helped him get the rescued girl into the craft.

"Hawk came over the radio. They're coming back in five, with the seized boxes of weapons. How's the girl?"

Shahrukh recognized the voice. It was the one they called River Rat.

"She's going to need medical attention," he said.

"Serious?"

"I've placed something on the wound to stop the bleeding, but she's lost a lot of blood. Get ready to transport her where she can be out of harm. I don't think the base will be able to take care of her injuries. Is everyone on the team coming back?"

"Affirmative, no injuries. Yet."

Shahrukh nodded and tucked the girl closer for a few moments, pulling his coat over her tightly. She was refusing to turn her head.

"Minah, these people will need you to speak in English where we are going. It's okay if it's just a little English because I'm sure they'll have interpreters. They're going to help you. I cannot stay, do you hear me?"

"Why can't you stay?"

"Because I have something I have to do. You will let the Americans take you away from here and live a happy life. You will be safe."

There was a pause.

"Okay," she finally said, in English. "Will...I...see you again?"

"*Insha'Allah*," Shahrukh replied. "God willing."

He opened the hatch. There was someone there.

"Ah, Kit," he said. "I have someone for you but you mustn't frighten her with your questions right now."

"Minah! Thank God." Kit moved things around. "Put her here. I'll take care of her."

"Kit?" Minah sounded grateful she recognized someone else.

"Please do not scream when you see her," he continued in a low voice. "And...maybe ask permission before you use that camera."

"What?" Kit asked.

He placed Minah next to Kit. "They cut off her nose." He could feel Kit's shock in the silence that followed. He continued, "She's all right but she needs medical attention as soon as possible. Don't make her cry again. She's trying to breathe through her mouth and not her nose. It's clogged up. Can you handle this?"

"O...Okay. All right. I...yes," Kit said, her voice growing stronger. "Yes, close the hatch. I'll take care of it."

"Good. I have full confidence you can handle this."

After all, he'd seen how determined she'd been, taking care of that SEAL of hers when he should have been out of commission hours and hours ago. Yet, the man was alive and out there doing his duty.

Lucky fellow.

Meanwhile, he had his own duty. He was going to kill the bastard who cut off Minah's nose himself.

* * *

The boat ride back to base was uneventful. Lucas was glad Kit opted to stay where she was. Safer. One never knew when a hostile decided to appear by the banks and start shooting. They stayed mostly quiet, keeping a watchful eye. They had a whole load of seized weapons to show any inquiry into their decision to attack the insurgents again after last night's successful raid to retrieve The Cob.

That episode seemed so long ago. It was the nature of life in the theatre, though. Things could move fast; lives could be taken just like that. Or, things could slow down to a plodding pace, hours that would turn into days of waiting for action. The last forty-eight hours fell into the former bracket.

River Rat had filled him in on what Shahrukh had told them before he left. That poor kid. He hadn't really checked in on their female passengers since they were in a hurry to get out of there. He'd knocked on the entryway and Kit had confirmed they were fine. He couldn't imagine the horror and pain of being thirteen and being disfigured like that. All of the guys who had been out in the battle zone had grown silent when they heard the report. He had a feeling he knew where Shahrukh had gone off to and he fucking approved.

Back at the secured area of the river, they disembarked quickly. It was already lit up and a larger than normal group was waiting for them. Medics. Vivi V-Z and Amber Hutchens. Other personnel to help account for the "confiscated" weapons. And some civilians he didn't recognize.

Hawk signaled the men to move a bit further away to give Kit and Minah room to get to Vivi. The medics, having been alerted of Minah's condition, were ready with beds and equipment. Jazz and a few of his team mates went to stand in front of the civilians and Lucas could hear some arguments coming from that direction.

Kit emerged from the hatch first, dirty, disheveled and so damn beautiful. He wanted to snatch her up and kiss her for a good long time. Then the young girl with her stood up very slowly. Since he was still on the boat to help them out, he was the first to see her face.

He stopped himself from uttering the angry curses that rose to his lips. He clenched his jaw and willed himself to look normal as they approached. Where her nose used to be, there was just a bloody mess with two black holes.

Someone had wiped most of the blood off but the red dried smears were horrific evidence of the torture she went through. Quickly he pulled out a hanky from his pocket and handed it to Kit. She shot him a grateful look before turning to Minah.

"Here you go. My friends will take care of you, okay?"

Minah nodded, holding Lucas' hanky in front of her disfigured face.

The moment they stepped off, the medics took over. Lucas stood to one side as Vivi, Amber and an interpreter took over. Urgent orders passed between the medics as they put Minah onto the bed and began checking on her vitals.

"Hey, Kit! Kit!" Someone called out.

Lucas turned in the direction of the civilians. Kit also swerved around.

"Sean? Sean!" She glanced quickly at Lucas and mouthed 'be right back' before trotting off to her colleagues.

So that was Sean and her media team. He vaguely remembered them at the morning fight now. He frowned as he caught the gist of the argument going on. Sean was protesting the fact Jazz wouldn't allow them closer to Minah.

"This lieutenant won't let us talk to Minah and take photos," Lucas heard him say to Kit. "It's part of the interview. Go take some pictures."

Kit shook her head. "No, Sean. It's not the right time," she said. "Minah is very traumatized. I think...we're going to need permission from her to take any more pictures."

"She's all bloodied up, Kit! We need the visuals to show in our article. You know it'd help our readers to understand the problems of..."

"Sean!" Kit interrupted. "Not tonight. Believe me. The article will be horrible enough without the pictures of Minah's condition."

"What if I make it an order?" Sean asked.

Lucas walked toward them. He wasn't going to allow this Sean fellow to threaten Kit, although he seemed more frustrated than angry.

"Is that a threat?" Kit asked.

Sean sighed. "No. It's been a fucking long day, waiting and not knowing whether you're all right. But we're missing a good story here, Kit."

"We aren't. We have a lot of material and I have a first person account. Me."

Sean nodded, then looked at Lucas standing behind Kit. He gave a small smile and pointed a finger. "Well. Is *that* a threat?"

Kit looked back, gave Lucas a frown, and turned back to Sean. "No."

"But I could be," Lucas said in a mild voice.

"Ah, more like a guard dog," Sean said, his head cocked slightly as he studied the two of them. "You must be the SEAL who ran off after Kit. I was told you two know each other. How about an interview about a certain raid? No names, of course. I've talked to your Lieutenant here and..."

Kit shook her head. "Sean, go stand over there and we'll discuss this in a few minutes. Please." Then she turned to Lucas again. "*You* aren't well. *You* go back there with the waiting doctors and let them take care of you. And here, you're supposed to drink this down. Now, please. It's been over an hour since your last one. You have quite a few more of these to go."

"Go, Cumber," Jazz, who had been quietly watching, said, amusement thickening his Cajun accent. "You should follow orders. After all, I was ordered by my wife to come here to prevent the reporters from interrupting her. Look, Hawk's heading over here now. He's probably been sent by Amber to stop making a racket. What are we SEALs to do but obey the women?"

The little jibe brought the level of tension down considerably.

"I heard that," Hawk said, when he reached them. "Cumber, you heard your orders. Don't worry. Kit will be there soon because she has more vials to feed you."

It was said in that easy, relaxed way his commander always conveyed, but it was nonetheless an order. He was to report to Medic. Lucas sighed. He'd hoped to avoid another fucking check-up, especially now that he felt one hundred percent better. The looks his two commanders gave him were loud and clear, though.

With a sigh, he waved his surrender to Kit, turned and trudged off to the waiting medics.

An hour later, he was still being checked by the base doctor. He sat impatiently, waiting for Kit. She was supposed to show up with the next vial of that magic cocktail. He didn't care about that. He just wanted her there with him.

"How long, doc?" He asked.

"Your heart rate is irregular. We don't like the second test results, so this is going to take a while, Branson. Lieutenant McMillan told me you've been drinking some kind of herbal concoction, that the base of this poison is castor oil, is that right?"

Lucas shrugged. "Right."

"Castor oil is also the base ingredient used to make ricin. You're showing similar symptoms of ricin poisoning."

"I didn't ingest the poison," Lucas quickly pointed out.

The doctor nodded. "I said symptoms. I don't have any idea what the poison is and we have to get a biopsy to be more conclusive."

"Of my wound? Shit."

"What? You get stabbed and called it a nick. Now you're acting like a pussy because we want to nick some bits of flesh off you? Should be like a paper cut, right? What's the hurry? Is it your girlfriend you're having a hard-on for?"

"Absolutely," Lucas drawled back. "Just move my big hard-on out of the way before you start cutting anything, okay?"

The doctor laughed. "That's the Cumber I'm used to." He took off his gloves. "I'll go get ready for the...minor...procedure. Meanwhile, your girlfriend is outside. I've taken a sample of that concoction of hers for testing too. I'm going to talk to your commanders and teammates to tell them you'll be here overnight for a kidney flush. Also, no pissing. You know that means a tube up your dick, right?"

Fucking asshole wanted to hear him cry. "Yeah, right, okay, thank you. Please tell Lieutenant McMillan I need to talk to him." He needed to report to Hawk about that other truck and the little boy. But first, please, just send Kit in here before he ripped all these needles out of his arm and get to her. He wanted to make sure she was okay.

After the doctor left, Lucas glared at the shut door. The doorknob finally turned and Kit burst in. She had cleaned up and changed her clothes. She took one look at him and burst into tears, running to the side of his bed. He held her with his free arm.

"What's wrong?" He asked, now truly worried.

Her tears were hot against his bare chest. "Just seeing you," she replied.

"I don't look that bad. Hey, it's okay." He stroked her hair. Must be delayed shock. It'd been a long day for his girl. "Everything's going to be fine, even for that young kid. Facial reconstruction would take care of her nose, you'll see. I'm sure..."

"It's not just that," Kit said, her voice muffled. "Just seeing you here made me realize how close I was to losing you. Don't lie about your condition like that again."

"It's part of my job, baby. Everything is dangerous." Including a knife shallowly. embedded in his belt. "We could have died from that grenade coming at us, remember? I was terrified about your safety all day."

Actually, he remembered feeling euphoric after the grenade hit the van and didn't explode. He would always remember Kit dancing her victory hustle. He'd wanted to marry her then.

"Well, like you're so fond of saying, I'm fine. I can take care of myself too. I took care of you," she told him airily, then dangled the vial in front of his nose. "Drink this down, get better, and maybe we can do a lot more spelunking."

He choked. "Spelunking?"

She grinned slyly, her cheeks still damp from her tears. "You know, cave exploration."

He laughed. The woman was his soul mate. "I love you," he told her softly.

"Is this the part where I tell you I love you back?" She teased.

"No, you're to say, 'I love you more and will never sing Airborne Ranger songs to you ever again."

She laughed and snuggled closer. "Can I stay here all night? I don't want to go out to deal with Sean until tomorrow."

She could stay forever by his side. Lucas moved over. She climbed up next to him. "Stay," he said, lowering his head, "and that's an order."

"I do love you," she whispered.

She lifted up her pretty face and met his kiss. He pushed his tongue inside her soft mouth, taking his time to taste her. Her tongue explored his as her hands reached up and laced behind his neck. The sweet taste of her was all the antidote he'd ever need. He reached around and cupped her soft breast—a perfect fit for his hand, he noted—rubbing the material over the nipple. He groaned. Braless.

Damn doctor better not return that quickly. Or like he'd promised earlier, his hard on was going to be in the way.

* * *

Shahrukh pulled at the yarn, breaking it as it meandered through the cave passages. He bent down to pick one end and started rolling the thread into a ball. A noise alerted him and after a pause, he continued his task.

"I see you've picked up a new hobby."

The husky voice, unexpected as a sudden breeze, floated from the shadows, away from the lantern light. It could move or freeze people, that voice. He'd yet to learn how to do that. Number Nine's effect on people made him a fascinating weapon to study.

"I've changed my mind," he said, concentrating on his chore. "Sending you here to clean up was a mistake."

He had just done his own version of cleaning up. That undertaking was eminently less peaceful than rolling yarn into a ball. He heard movement again and then the shadowy figure appeared. He stopped and studied the man, who returned the favor.

"You look strange in our native garb, Jed," Shahrukh observed lightly, "but the stubble does add a movie-star quality."

"And you look a lot less than your usual serene self," Jed said, his strange silver gaze sweeping him from head to toe. Besides the blood on his clothes giving away his recent activities, he was sure Jed had his ways of finding out what had happened. "Killing in cold blood doesn't settle well, does it? Was it the clean up you sent me for?"

Shahrukh shook his head. "No. It was personal."

"Even more dangerous to the soul."

A very profound statement from an assassin. Shahrukh looked at the other man for another long moment. "It had to be done. This other assignment can wait. Like I said, I've changed my mind." He thought of the woman lying in a coma back at Center, the one person who had started to make his friend feel again. "Go home. Be with her. She needs you." When Jed turned and walked away, he continued, "What if Hell dies while you're doing your job? You'll regret it. Don't you...care?"

Jed paused in mid-step but didn't turn around. "Rukh. It's a pattern in my life. My hands are too bloodstained from death. They contaminate those I...care about. There is no better punishment, so I'll just do my job. I'll catch up with you in Karakoram. I think I might go and watch your friend Zerya for a while. An interesting woman."

Shahrukh didn't stop his fellow COS commander as he strode off down the tunnel. He would return soon enough because he was Number Nine, the one in his unit who finished a Virus mission. He knew Shahrukh would give him the assignment sooner or later. That last jibe was meant to distract him from probing any further about his mental condition.

Zerya was in no danger and she was capable of making decisions and taking care of herself. Besides, Jed's mind was on another far more interesting woman, one who could *move* a cold bastard like him.

Punishment? That word carried a lot of emotional baggage. His friend was in worse shape than he'd thought.

"Karakoram," he murmured in agreement. Where the soulless go to trade.

CHAPTER FIFTEEN

Charleston,
Two months later

Kit took pictures of her friend Lulu and Mink sharing a huge glass of some kind of blue mixed drink. Sitting across the booth table, they both had their lips pursed on the rim of the glass in between them. Right at the moment she clicked the button, Mink made one of his godawful faces, his mouth grotesquely wide open, one eye half-shut. Predictably, Lulu squealed.

"Can't you just take a normal photo with me?" She asked in disgust. "Every photo we have together looks like I'm sitting next to a monster."

Mink grinned. "I think I look great in those photos."

"Kit, do something!" Her friend pleaded.

Kit shook her head. Mink was a gorgeous man, with a killer smile that could melt snow, but he was a member of an elite Navy SEAL team. She suspected his playfulness was partly because of his job and an unwillingness to have his face identified and partly because he loved to tease Lulu. Maybe mostly the latter because she noticed Mink had the biggest smile whenever Lulu got riled up.

"Please, Mink," Kit said, smiling sweetly. "It's Valentine's Day, not Halloween. Let's make an exception and give Lulu a photo to remember this day, without the faces. I know about your fear of your perfect model looks being captured in a still, but I promise, this one will be in a private album for just us girls."

"Aw, Mink, relent a bit, dude. Kit is begging," Dirk, who was leaning against the far end glass window so Kit could take her picture, said. "Also, hear my pleas. I'm hungry."

Mink let out an exaggerated sigh and looked across at Lucas, sitting next to her. "With your permission, sir, may I have a smiley photo with your sister?"

"Hey!" Lulu huffed. "Why do you always ask him first, dammit?"

"Well, seeing that it's Valentine's Day," Lucas drawled. "You have my permission."

"Thank you, Cumber," Mink said then grinned at Kit. He pushed the big glass away and scooted closer to Lulu. Putting an arm around her shoulders, his grin turned into a charming smile. "Hurry up, this one's free. Next one's going to cost ya."

"Okay!" Kit said. "Lulu, say 'cheese!'"

She leaned forward to get a closer shot and just as her forefinger came down to click on the button, Mink turned Lulu into his arms. A startled Lulu grabbed his shoulder to steady herself. He leaned forward and planted a deep kiss on her friend's lips.

Click.

"Oh my! Rhett! You do give a damn!" Kit teased, affecting Miss Clementine's very southern accent. "Classic pose! Looks good, Lulu!"

Her friend straightened up and pushed Mink away. Her face was flushed and her voice, just a little breathy. "The last time he was Rhett Butler he had two straws up his nose for a moustache. One cannot unsee that in one's brain."

"The kiss was meant to befuddle you, my dear."

"Frankly, I don't give a damn," Lulu sniped back pertly.

Everyone chuckled. Kit set her slim camera on the window ledge, along with her smart phone. With those two children across the table, she didn't want to chance any of her of electronic stuff getting wet.

This Valentine's Day was perfect. The Stooges had the rest of the week off and had come to town and she'd just finished her interview with Minah, who was still in a special military hospital in Virginia. Lucas had kissed her senseless the moment she'd arrived at the airport.

They'd gone off to say hi to her mom and dad who had met Lucas when he was rehabilitating in the hospital in Germany. They got on great, although dad managed to slide in a couple of SEAL jokes which Lucas had politely taken in good humor.

Yay, both sets of Parental Units had given their approval.

They had all first met in Germany. They'd actually flown there to see Kit when she'd called them up about not coming home with the media team for a few more weeks. After hearing her story and how Lucas' poisoning had a setback and needed more sophisticated care, Kit's father had called in some favors and before she knew it, both her parents were knocking at her room in the military hospital. It so happened Lucas' parents were by his bedside too and their families had the chance to bond over her boyfriend's injury.

She leaned against Lucas' arm. It'd been a month and a half since his hospital stay but she was still worried about him. The doctors had assured her his kidney wasn't badly damaged but still, they hadn't known about the dangerous aftereffects of the poison, so how could they know if he was one hundred percent?

Lucas, of course, was just glad to be out. He hated everything at the hospital. He hated being the only one on his team sick and was the worst patient ever. He hated the hospital food. He hated being confined in the room with needles sticking out of him. He hated to be in the hospital skirt, as he called it. Boy, hate was not a strong enough word.

All she cared about was he was here with her. But just in case, she'd kept that card Mr. Shahrukh had given her.

Whoever he was, he'd saved Lucas' life and even if she might not need to ask him for any antidote potion any more, she did want to thank him.

It was so typical of the Stooges, though, to choose Chinese food for Valentine's Day. The restaurant had a Valentine Special and the owner, who came out to greet them effusively like they were old friends, placed all the orders himself.

Lucas had just shrugged and said, "Bring it on. I need real food after the last two months."

When the food arrived, Kit wanted to giggle. Everything was served on pink plates. There were artfully cut and arranged pink vegetable and fruit at the side of each dish. The guys were hugely amused and Lucas didn't seem too bothered.

"Pink cucumber, dude!" Mink said. "You'll never live it down."

"Look at that pink pearly thing. Are those peas?"

"If you wait a bit, all the dishes will be out soon," the owner said. "In China, it's tradition to have all the dishes in the middle and everyone shares the meal, like a happy family."

Lucas nodded. "Everything looks great. I love it," he declared.

Kit stared at him. He seemed normal. Actually, he looked freaking hot in his shirt and pants. His hair had grown longer and was slicked back. She loved the way it curled around the collar and wished he didn't have to cut those pretty locks off ever again. Being in special operations had some advantages. The men sometimes had to blend in with the local fighters and her brothers had returned home looking very unmilitary a time or two before.

As they waited, conversation drifted to the usual banter and then the men were deep in discussion about the call that just came in from Hawk. She knew, from what Lucas divulged, it had to do with that strange little boy who was shouting at them. Something about a message and deciphering it. Because the kid was yelling military slang,

Lucas could remember most of them. Hawk had agreed that it merited a closer look and would point it out in his report to the Admiral. Was that boy really giving some kind of message? She smiled secretly. Lucas didn't know it but she'd jotted down a lot of what sounded like military slang coming from that boy into her notebook. She'd have to sit down and look through her pile of notes and find it. Perhaps there could be a new story in there.

Already, Minah's story was becoming a sensation. Sean had insisted on giving her a lot of the credit even though the prep work was a team effort. She'd become part of the story now and a connection to Minah, who had bravely given her permission to take photographs of her face. The young girl was still without a nose but her attitude was amazingly positive. Her caretakers and staff of doctors had taken the effort to make her comfortable and she was excited about finally being in the United States and perhaps meeting Malala, the other Afghan girl who was shot in the head by the Taliban.

The next article in the series would be about Minah's future. There had been thousands of emails and letters offering help and adoption. As Sean said, "one hell of a story there too."

Her own account, minus certain details, had also been broadcasted on several Internet news service. She'd declined many of interviews about herself, preferring to concentrate on Minah's and her fellow countrywomen's plight. Even Sean had agreed to hold off putting the details about the weapons cache after Admiral Madison had personally called him at the office. She found out later that he'd been promised to be part of the next SEAL-related operation as an embedded journalist. She'd like to meet the Admiral one day. That song Lucas had taught her had made her very curious about his background.

So many amazing stories to tell, her cup runneth over. She was learning, though, to let her story speak through imagery. She might hold back a few details, but her photos documented the truth. Minah's face. The blotches of blood on Lucas' uniform. The deep new scar he now had on the side of his body. The dark and narrow cavern. The burnt-out shell that was the school. Contrast those with the magnificent beauty of the Swat Valley she'd taken from the treetop. The smiling children accepting their gifts. The picture she took of the hustle and bustle in the Mingora marketplace. Sean's stories were hard-hitting, brilliant pieces but she felt she'd added a more intimate perspective to their article.

Kit looked around at her friends. When the food arrived, she wanted to take a picture of all those gorgeous dishes to remember today. Lucas was with her and these were his and her best friends. Perfect moment. As she reached for her phone, her elbow hit her tiny camera and sent it off the ledge. She tried to catch it but it bounced off the plastic seat and fell between the booth and the wall.

The others didn't notice as she tried to push her hand in the small space to get at her camera. Damn it. She couldn't find it. Not wanting to disturb their conversation and without much thought, she slid down the booth seat in one nimble move. Being small had its advantage. She could fit anywhere.

On her hands and knees, she peered down but found there was no opening under the booth, just solid wood. A moment of panic assailed her. How the hell was she going to get her camera out of that? Then she caught sight of the vinyl string that was attached to the side of her camera. Thank God. It was just jammed between the seat and the wall and if she was very careful, she could get it out of there before it fell all the way down inside the booth.

She curled two fingers into the crack and used her nails to slowly coax the string forward. It wobbled towards her unsteadily.

"Come to mama," she crooned. "Yes, yes. That's a good boy. Yes!"

Her camera back safely in her possession, she turned and slid back up on her seat. Easy-peasy. The whole thing couldn't have taken longer than a minute and the others wouldn't even noti...silence greeted her.

Kit glanced around at her friends. Every pair of eyes was on her. Even the waiter and the owner, who were standing by the table with bowls of rice in their hands, ready to serve, were looking at her bemusedly.

Lucas was giving her the most amused smile, an eyebrow cocked above eyes shiny with laughter.

"What?" Kit asked, holding up her camera as explanation. "I was just..."

Huh. The others had heard her telling something to "come to mama," followed by her excited "yes, yes yes." Oh, Lord. She blushed.

"What was all that about?" asked Mink slyly.

"That was my ordering today's special," Lucas replied, his smile turning sinfully wicked as he gave her a wink.

Everyone started to laugh. Kit turned redder.

"Oh, my God, Kit," Lulu choked in between fits of laughter. "If only you had seen our faces when we heard you under the table. You'll be hearing about this for a while."

Kit stuck out her tongue. "Shut up," she said rudely and spooned some chicken onto her rice. "Shut up and eat."

Lucas chuckled and his big hand scratched her back. "One day—"

"Don't even think about it and don't say your dirty thoughts out loud," she ordered, knowing the direction of his mind too well. She took a bite of her food. "Oh, wow! This is delicious, guys."

That managed to change the subject, something for which she was eminently grateful. Not that they would forget the incident. She was sure it would be brought up as a reminder of that Valentine dinner with the pink dishes.

Everyone happily devoured the food. Even the fortune cookies were pink and she took a picture of them because it was just too funny. Lucas was going to have a big bill, but when she offered to help out with it, he just gave her one of those male looks. He pushed a fortune cookie onto her plate, cracked his open and read it out loud.

"Do not insult man who eats pink cucumber," he said. "What does yours say?"

She picked hers up. As she broke hers open, she saw the flash from Lulu's camera and looked up at her friend.

"Hey, tit for tat," Lulu said. "I want a picture of you and Lucas staring at a pink fortune cookie. Come on, hurry up!"

Kit looked up and smiled at Lucas because she wanted to have a nice picture with him. He had an odd little smile on his lips, like he was enjoying what he was looking at, and it sent a delicious shiver down her spine. Oh, they had better be alone very, very soon or she was liable to attack—

She glanced down at her cookie with a frown. What was this? She unwrapped the small piece of paper.

"Oh, my God," she said.

She looked up at Lucas. His smile had turned tender. She looked down at the diamond ring, totally speechless.

"Read your fortune," Lucas said, his voice soft and impatient.

She picked up the paper and read out loud, "Will you marry me?"

"Yes, I will," Lucas replied and pulled her into his arms. "I love you, Kit-Ling, my Cupcake, *moi melenkei kotonok*. I want to be with you always. Come to papa!"

She just laughed and wrapped her arms around the muscular body. "Yes!" she yelled out. "Yes! Yes! Yes! And you never told me what that phrase meant."

"It's Russian. You're the nerd, go Google it," Lucas said. "Kiss me and I'll tell you later."

Kit complied, ignoring her friends' hoots and teasing, locking her lips passionately with her very own SEAL. He kissed her possessively, taking his time, as usual, showing her with action rather than words how much he loved and wanted her.

"A perfect Valentine all caught on video," announced Lulu smugly. "SEALed with a kiss! Haha."

"Dude, check out that rock."

"I did. I helped steam the darn cookie open, you idiot, while you and Lulu were fooling around."

"Hey, we were in charge of—"

Everyone was talking at once but Kit didn't hear a thing. She was too busy kissing her warrior on the most memorable Valentine's Day ever.

THE END

I hope you enjoyed Lucas and Kit's story. If you want to read about the other SEALs, here are their titles:

Jazz and Vivi's story is in PROTECTOR
Hawk and Amber's story is in HUNTER
Reed (Joker) and Lily's story is in SLEEPER
Zone and Rebecca's story is in (Her Secret) PIRATE –
a short story

Research notes

1) *Malala Yousafzai's story can be found in many news articles. She was a student activist advocating education when the Taliban shot her in the head. She has written a book about her life.

2) Many women in Afghanistan and Pakistan and their shared border remain uneducated and dependent. There have been some positive changes, including the recent appointment of a female elder in the *jirga*, but there are still many violent crimes committed against young women. Through newspaper accounts and research, I've weaved my own stories about the victims, but the crimes are real, with very little justice handed out.

3) The Kurdish *Peshmerga* troops do allow women into their army. I am very fascinated by these strong and fiercely independent women. Their stories call out to be told. The recent assassination of three female leaders brought worldwide attention and of course, many conspiracies abound around their deaths.

4) The references to The Game is from my serial stories about a secret treasure hunting organization called The Temple. The books are titled The Game and The Pawn. You will find unexpected connections of "Ahmin" and Lucas Branson in those stories.

5) Downed Stealths and stolen Stealth parts are, unfortunately, real. A paint with a radar-cloaking agent is also real. My conspiracy theory putting those two items together, hopefully, not so real.

6) *Moi malenkei kotonok* is anglicized Russian for "my little kitten." Wait until Kit finds out and calls him "my big

pink Cucumber" in Chinese. But that's another story, I'm afraid.

About the Author

Gennita Low writes sexy military and techno spy-fi romance. She also co-owns a roof construction business and knows 600 ways to kill with roofing tools as well as yell at her workers in five languages. A three-time Golden Heart finalist, her first book, Into Danger, about a SEAL out-of-water, won the Romantic Times Reviewers Choice Award for Best Romantic Intrigue. Besides her love for SEALs, she works with an Airborne Ranger who taught her all about mental toughness and physical endurance. Gennita lives in Florida with her mutant poms and one chubby squirrel.

To learn more about Gennita, visit www.Gennita-Low.com, www.rooferauthor.blogspot.com and www.facebook.com/gennita

Other Books by Gennita Low

~ ~ COS Commando Series ~ ~
BIG BAD WOLF

~ ~ Crossfire Series ~ ~
PROTECTOR
HUNTER
SLEEPER
HER SECRET PIRATE (short story in SEAL of my Dreams) & also available separately
WARRIOR

~ ~ Secret Assassins (S.A.S.S.) ~ ~
INTO DANGER
FACING FEAR
TEMPTING TROUBLE

~ ~ Sex Lie & Spies Serials ~ ~
THE GAME
THE PAWN

~.~.Super Soldier Spy ~ ~
VIRTUALLY HIS
VIRTUALLY HERS

~ ~ Children's books as "Gennita" ~ ~

A SQUIRREL CAME TO STAY

CPSIA information can be obtained at www.ICGtesting.com
Printed in the USA
LVOW08s0248090115

422113LV00001B/128/P